NEXT

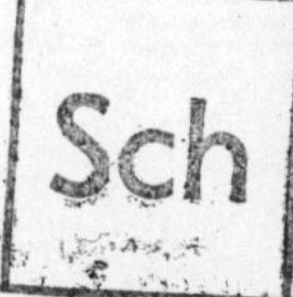

NEXT

edited by

Keith Gray

ANDERSEN PRESS

First published in 2012 by
Andersen Press Limited
20 Vauxhall Bridge Road
London SW1V 2SA
www.andersenpress.co.uk

British Library Cataloguing in Publication Data available.

ISBN 978 1 84939 300 3

Printed and bound by CPI Group (UK) Ltd, Croydon, CR0 4YY

CONTENTS

STARBURSTING 1
by Julie Bertagna

GREEN FIELDS 25
by Jonathan Stroud

'THESE ARE THE YOLKS, FOLKS!' 55
by Philip Ardagh

SURFACE WATER 77
by Gillian Philip

THE RECEIVING END 103
by Malorie Blackman

THE FALLEN 125
by Sally Nicholls

CAN'T YOU SLEEP? 151
by Frank Cottrell Boyce

BURYING BARKER 173
by Keith Gray

STARBURSTING

Julie Bertagna

STARBURSTING

I never expected to lose you, Jamie, not then. And not like that, on the night I turned seventeen.

Well, how could I?

I was a girl with my heart on fire.

I had other plans.

It was one of those summer nights when you think you'll live forever. Life was just opening up for both of us.

Exams were over. You'd just passed your driving test, first time. It was the night before my birthday. We'd pretended you'd booked a local restaurant and wanted to drive me there in style. You hadn't. That's what you told your mum so you'd get to borrow her car. We promised we'd stick to the quiet suburban streets if she'd let us have her beloved red Mini for the night.

We lied.

The second we'd turned out of your street, onto the main road, we revved past the Spar shop where the usual bored slump of underage teens sprawled on the grass verge, squabbling over the can of beer they'd bribed a local tramp to buy. They turned to watch us like a five-headed creature, all arms and legs and sullen eyes. I saw Ross, my younger brother, and we exchanged a silent pact – I wouldn't grass him up about the beer if he forgot he'd seen us speeding out towards the country.

We headed up into the hills where the evening sky wasn't boxed in by ranks of roofs but stretched on forever, all fire and iridescence, as far as we could see.

I'd promised I'd spend my birthday with my family, like I always did. I'd sulked a bit, trying to get out of the usual trek to the local Chinese. It was the first birthday I'd had a proper boyfriend and I wanted to spend it with you, Jamie. But Mum got all emotional. '*You've got the rest of your life to have birthdays with boyfriends,*' she moaned. '*And you'll be off to university after the summer. This might be the last birthday we'll have you all to ourselves, Cass.*'

So I gave in. I did a deal. I bagged the night before – as long as I could stay out past midnight with you. Then we'd at least have a bit of my birthday together. It always bugged me that I had to be in by half eleven on normal week nights, as if I might turn into a pumpkin by twelve. Well, it was either that, I told Mum and Dad calmly, or I'd spend my whole birthday night with you and they wouldn't see me at all. Dad shrugged and said it sounded fair enough to him, so Mum was out voted. I got a one o'clock curfew and my Plan was on course.

You know, if I'd done my usual thing and got into a strop, Mum and I would've ended up in a fight, she'd have put her foot down, and it would've been, 'All right, young lady, birthday or not you can forget it – you're not going out at all!'

And none of it would have happened. Think of that.

But I kept cool. I had a Plan, and nothing was going to spoil this night for you and me.

The city blazed behind us as we raced out onto the winding country roads, the tower blocks rising like tall flames from the ashen dusk of the streets as the sunset turned all their windows to fire. I glimpsed the red glare in the wing mirror and thought it looked as if some great catastrophe had struck and turned the city into a burning pyre.

I never guessed that disaster really was just seconds away.

The stupidest thing I've ever done in my life was slip off my seatbelt so that I could lean over to kiss you, as we swerved into a tight bend. Out of the corner of my eye I saw one of those big ugly cars that look like black tanks heading towards us. Even at that point, it might not have happened if the couple in the black tank weren't in the middle of some argument... Maybe she'd have turned the wheel a second earlier and both of us might have got out alive.

Blackness is all I remember next. Thudding darkness. A massive impact, an explosion of pain that seared through every cell of my body.

I must've hurtled through the smashed window of the Mini. Light seared out of the darkness and the sky seemed to open its arms to me as I fell into a never-ending twilight.

I'd killed you.

That was my first and only thought when I saw the crushed and bloodied mess they were loading into the ambulance. It was all my fault. I'd taken your mind off the road.

Tugging presences urged me to let you go, kept trying to drag me away from you. But I broke free. I would not leave you. Ever.

It was supposed to be the best night of our lives. You couldn't die.

And you didn't, not then. You still whispered to me, your voice all broken as if you'd swallowed some of the shattered glass that was everywhere – in your hair, among your blood and tears, all over your mum's Mini and the road. You promised me that everything was going to be all right. This couldn't happen, not to us, you said. We'd so many dreams still to live.

The ambulance took you away. I went with you. Nothing could stop me. I never left your side, not for a second, even in the hospital where I could barely reach you through the medics and tubes and bandages and painkilling drugs that made you look right through me as if I were a pane of glass.

Later, when streams of relatives and friends came to stroke your hair and hold your hand and cry over you, I still couldn't break through the invisible barrier that seemed to have slammed down between us. Were you angry with me? Did you blame me? The only answer in your eyes was pain. Last of all, worst of all, was when my own family came and sat by your bedside. Their waves of grief crashed all around me, and I couldn't bear it. Everyone seemed to forget I was there.

The truth gradually engulfed me.

I *wasn't* there.

That's why you looked through me, all of you.

I was the thing that had looked like a mashed pumpkin on the bonnet of the mangled Mini. The woman driver of the ugly black tank had drawn back from the sight, moaning, her hands over her mouth as her husband eased the bloodied mess of you from the driver's seat. It was *me* the ambulance people covered from head to toe in a white sheet by the roadside while they raced you off to hospital.

I was the one who was dead.

Being dead isn't what you might think. Our cat used to bring dead things home as presents – birds, mice, baby squirrels. When we buried them, I could feel that all the energy was gone from the poor little bodies. But you can't tell what death really is from a lifeless body. I'm not Cassie Grant anymore, caught inside a body and brain. I'm not a ghost girl. How can I tell you what I am?

There's nothing left of me.

And yet I'm everything, now.

I'm the energy that drives the universe. Without me, you couldn't live. I am what you once were and will be again, some day.

I was so clueless back then. I thought I could make my life happen the way I wanted it to. Like my Big Plan that fatal night. Jamie, did you even guess? You only had enough money to buy me a small gift so you'd thought up another, special present for me. *The kind a girl gets from a maths geek*, you joked. I niggled away until I got it out of you, just in case it was something I'd hate and I'd have to put on a pleased face. But it was a sweet idea. You'd drive me out to your best star-gazing spot, way beyond the light pollution of the city, and show me the stunning constellation that was my namesake: Queen

Cassiopeia's sparkling star crown.

I was actually Cassidy, named after a cowboy in my Dad's all-time favourite film, but I didn't tell you. I liked it that, whenever you looked up at the stars and saw Queen Cass, you wanted to think of me. And I wanted you to think of me, always. Even though we'd soon go separate ways – I'd study languages and travel the world; you'd do astronomy and explore the universe – I was determined to keep you, somehow.

A little box wrapped in shiny silver paper sat on the back seat of the car, beside your telescope. You'd even organised clear skies for my birthday, you said, and your smile filled me with the scary wild excitement I get on a roller-coaster ride. You wanted it to be an unforgettable night. And it would be. You didn't yet know it, but your real birthday gift to me would be you. That was my Big Plan.

I'd done one of my checklists, the kind I always do before a heavy exam or a holiday. But I hadn't pinned this one on my bedroom wall; it was hidden away, locked in my phone organiser.

New knickers ✓ (Sultry black or sexy red. Crucial choice. See how I feel on the night.)

Feet and body scrub ✓ (Especially feet – hate my toes.)

Leg and bikini wax ✓ (First ever – wow, sore!)

Steal Mum's new red sandals ✓ (There'll be hell if she finds out.)

Paint toe nails ✓ (Does it matter? Does a boy care about your toenails when he's having sex with you under the stars? DO NOT over co-ordinate red sandals, nails and knickers. Don't want to look like I'm trying too hard. Though I am.)

Condoms from café toilets ✓ (Took three cafés and gallons of caramel latte, but I finally got one.)

So I was all set. I loved you, Jamie, and I wanted to be part of you. I wanted you and me to be truly *us*.

Excitement thrummed inside me as I got ready that afternoon. I'd never felt so nervous and so – so *alive*. It just wasn't fair. How could I have died when I was so full of life?

I always hated maths. Just didn't see the point. I'd have wormy feelings in my stomach the night before a school test and by the time it came to the big exams I'd be a wreck. I'd look at a page full of numbers and symbols and feel my brain freeze. I dropped it as soon as I could. But if I hadn't been such a dimwit, we'd never have got together.

Everything that happened started at morning assembly when Mr Goring, a young maths teacher, whose idea of fun was a Sunday-morning maths challenge, announced he needed some guinea pigs for a research project by the Pi Club geeks. (He didn't actually say 'geeks', of course, but everyone knew they were.) The human brain, droned Boring Goring, was designed to understand the beauty of mathematical patterns. All that was stopping those who thought they couldn't do maths was a faulty circuit in the wiring of their brain, a simple electrical failure that the right electrician could fix.

'*Who*,' Mr Goring asked, his earnest face breaking into a geeky grin, '*would like to be a contestant in my "XY Factor" contest?*'

The mistake I made was to duck as he looked around the assembly hall for an example of a mathematically-challenged guinea pig. I was right in the middle of the second row and my 'hide' reflex immediately drew his eyes to me. As I shuffled up onto the stage, with the whole school chortling and heckling, I could feel strawberry-pink embarrassment flushing all over my face – which turned tomato-red when Mr Goring called out the name of my personal electrician.

You.

Jamie Raine.

You were the boy I adored from afar. The one I'd secretly followed home from school and dreamed about day and night, ever since you rescued me from a gang of kids who were trying to shove me into a pond of frogspawn when I was ten years old. You were the shining star of the *Pi Club*, more god-like than geek, with a smile that lit a fuse inside me. You were The One that was meant to be mine forever, I'd decided long ago, though you didn't know it then.

I could not believe my luck.

The sun streamed in molten beams through your living-room window that afternoon you took me to your house after school. My bare arm kept brushing yours as we sat close together on the sofa, giving me goose bumps, though I was too hot. You wanted to show me how an equation was like a cosmic poem, and scribbled half a page of symbols that told the story, you said, of how a star is born. Then you rambled on about exploding supernovae and imploding dwarf stars and how we were all made of stardust, when it came down to it, because everything that has ever existed in the universe came out of the Big Bang...

I was only half listening. I was watching you, drinking you in – the scent of just-eaten tangerine on your mouth, the metallic glint of sun on your dark hair, your blue eyes feverish as the ideas tumbled inside you.

Then you looked up at me. And I felt as if a hundred invisible little wires were connecting me to you and, somehow, we'd flicked a switch and a live current zipped through us both. It was too much.

I chickened out, trying to break the tension with a weak joke that my XY Factor was permanently challenged; my internal wiring was wonky beyond repair. I'd never understand all that stuff, not in a million years.

You didn't laugh. You didn't say a word. Just leaned in and kissed me, and you tasted of tangerine. We couldn't stop the kiss. We were burning up, I was imploding into you, you into me…

Now I get it. Finally, I understand everything you were trying to explain that day because all the equations of the universe are unfolding around me and through me now.

Jamie, the things I've done since I died you wouldn't believe.

I've whirled a hundred million light years, past trillions of stars. Hitched a ride on the glowing gas tail of a runaway star. I've spun on the spurs of Orion and the spirals of Andromeda, romped all through the Virgo supercluster, our tiny patch of the universe, among ten million superclusters…

I've become part of the magic of the universe. Me, Cassie Grant. Though I always *had* been, we all are, and I never knew. Does anyone?

But you did. You saw it in a page of symbols when you were seventeen.

After I died, I was disconnected from everything I'd known. But the grief that consumed you and my family – Jamie, it raked through me like a firestorm. I couldn't bear it. So I whirled away, deep into the universe where supernovas exploded into whirligigs of new galaxies. I got lost, for I don't know how long, among the constellations. Climbed luminous pillars of nebula clouds – seven-light-years high – giant nurseries of dust and gas and fountains of plasma, where new stars are born.

And I wanted you there. I wanted to share it all with you. But I was at the far edges of the universe and you were aeons away.

So I hurled myself back through the endless curves of space-time, back to our place in the cosmos. But Earth had become a strange place. I'd been gone too long, too far, and it no longer felt like home. Everything I knew was gone. Strange, armoured creatures crawled, lava mountains and boiling seas spumed like sherbet foam. Had I landed in a far future when human life was extinct? Or was I sunk deep in the past?

I plunged forward and backwards, spinning through time, searching through the vastness of history, until at long last I found you again, in the very moment I'd crashed out of your life, years ago.

And so I lived my own death twice. The first time as myself. This time through you. I became part of your grief, your very tears. I was in the sweat of your sleepless nights and in clammy moments of loneliness when no one could help you. Jamie, I was there. I wish I could have let you know, sent you some sign.

Sometimes I thought you felt my presence. Those nights you stood at your bedroom window, staring up at the star crown of Queen Cass, and I'd wrap myself around you in the only way I could... invisibly, soft as a ghost.

You burst from your grief suddenly one day, throwing it off like an old skin, as if you couldn't get rid of it fast enough. A letter had come in the post. You gave such a yell when you opened it that your parents turned white, dreading another calamity. But in the letter was the chance of a lifetime. You'd won a scholarship to follow your dreams – to study the universe and the stars.

You dragged your telescope out from under your bed and wiped off months of dust. Then you packed your bags and left the hard memories behind.

Now your life was full of new people, studies, fun. The time came when you found someone else. All wrapped up in her, your memories of me began to fade. You seemed to feel my presence less and less, and when you did I only made you shiver. I'd become something you needed to forget. This time I had to let you go.

My family's grief had bound them so tightly together I felt locked out of their lives too. Ross grew angry when I was around, as if my presence was a thorn in wounds that needed to heal. I wrenched myself away.

Once again I drifted through space, trying to work out the puzzle of my new existence. I sought out the other presences now. I'd been so wrapped up in myself I hadn't paid much attention before but they were there, around me. Sizzling energy fields and intelligences. From every corner of the universe, and all times. They'd been alive, once, too. Now they were cosmic wanderers like me.

What am I? I asked them. *What's the point of me?*

Death had not turned out to be what I'd imagined – in the brief moments I'd dared to wonder about it at all. Well, you try not to think about it, don't you? And you don't really believe it'll ever happen, not to you. I mean, how can *you* – all your thoughts and feelings and sensations and pulsing life – ever not *be*? But where did you get all that energy? Where were you before you were born?

Not being alive wasn't a blank nothingness, a void, an extinction of everything that was once me. I hadn't found God or landed up in heaven or some hellish place or passed through to a new dimension, not really, when I could still loiter about in the space and time I once lived. But I was useless. I was like some old song that everyone's forgotten, stuck on replay, the sound turned down so low that no one even hears. Just an energy cluster left behind by a body that's dead and gone. Yet I was still, in some bewildering sense, me.

I pleaded with the other presences to help me find out what I was. None of them knew. We were, all of us, lost and searching. Only a few, so dense with imploding energy they felt like the nebula clouds that birthed new stars, had any clue to the mystery of what we were or might become.

Just wait, they said. *It feels as though you're locked out on the wrong side of a closed window forever. But your time will come. And then you'll know what you're for. You'll find out why you're still here. Meanwhile, there's all of space and time to play with . . .*

Well, I'd already done that, hadn't I?

So then I had my dropout years. Furious, confused, at odds with the whole wide world, I went a bit crazy – chasing thrills, getting high. I spent several million lifetimes hurtling through black holes into unknown regions of the cosmos, losing myself in voids all across the wastes of space. I hung out with every scrap of dark, wrecking energy I could latch on to. We helter-skeltered through plasma fountains, blazed with the comets, kicked asteroids around the galaxies and stamped on the embers of a dying sun. Then we gate-crashed some worlds and burned them all out. Almost burned myself out too.

With my anger exhausted at last, I sunk into a sullen black strop. For about three hundred thousand years, or so...

Until something drew me to your place and time, drew me back to you. A magnetic force pulling me in, calling time on my reckless wanderings.

I rushed through folds of space-time until I found Earth, still glowing and spinning; a serene blue-green gem with its pearly moon. My own human life seemed like a barely remembered dream, yet it all came rushing back to me once I found my town, my old home. But that house was full of strangers now. Nothing was the same.

What year was it? Where were my parents? My brother?

Jamie, I couldn't find you.

Had your lifetime passed while I'd been on my cosmic rampage?

Grief hit me as hard as an asteroid storm. All I could do was follow the urgent force that still pulled. I let it take me over the oceans to the far side of the world. It swept me across deserts and forests, over mountains, rivers, cities and towns, until I came to a green park where a boy sat on a swing.

'Higher!' he shouted to the grandfatherly figure who was pushing him.

I knew the child's shining blue eyes, his beautiful smile.

It was you, Jamie, as a little boy.

I must have got my timing all wrong because if you were in your childhood that meant I was too. Did the mysterious twists and folds of space-time mean I could be alive – yet dead too?

But why were you here, on the other side of the world?

'Time to go, Ben!' called the old man, and he shivered though the afternoon sun was still warm. He looked over his shoulder and rubbed his arms as if he felt sudden goose bumps under his shirt.

The little boy, Ben, wasn't you.

Still I didn't know you, not even then. I was puzzled by the boy. It was only when the grandfather turned round that I saw the same eyes and smile as the child, but in an old face.

Then I understood.

You were the man, not the boy. While I'd been away, you'd grown old.

Pain was in every step you took, in your stiff and aching bones, even as you laughed and played with your grandson. You'd used up your human energy, that was all. I could feel it ebbing out of you those last days, and I knew all I could do – as you'd done in the last moments of my life – was stay close and promise you that everything would be all right, because we'd so many dreams still to live, the two of us. We'd so much left to do.

The night before you died Ben dragged you out of bed to look at a star-sizzled sky.

'There's Orion with his sword.' The little boy's breath misted the window as he pointed up. 'And there's the Big Dipper and the Seven Sisters and – and what else, Grandpa?'

'Who's the queen of the sky?' you prompted.

'Cass!' shouted Ben.

You gazed for a long moment at the twinkling crown of stars. And I knew you'd never forgotten me.

You have the look of someone listening very hard to a song that no one else in the room can hear. To the living ones around your bed, you seem to fade with every breath. But it's only human life that's seeping away as you make the final wrench and burst free of your worn-out body, casting off old skin and frail bones. The moment of your death releases an irresistible force, an energy field that pulls me towards it. Pulls you too.

All I am now is a nebulous trembling as you rush into me. At long last, after sixty human years and aeons wandering the universe, I get what I wanted.

I get you.

That's why I'm still here.

Finally, I understand the unsolved equation of myself. My life was snuffed out far too soon and, somehow, like a failed dwarf star, I didn't fuse – just didn't have enough energy to flare white-hot and transform into something altogether new on my own. I had to wait for you.

'The first step in the birth of a star,' you once told me, 'is to wait. There's aeons of waiting until a passing star, even an old star, fuses it with a shock wave of new energy. And then . . .' – you grinned and puffed out your cheeks, mimicking the explosion of a big bang – 'starburst!'

So that's what we're doing. Starbursting. All the energy that was once you and me is merging, fusing, burning together.

Becoming . . . *us*.

A blistering new cosmic poem.

I don't know what we are yet, but we've got all the time in the world to find out. There's infinity to explore. Where do we begin?

I think of all the things I want to show you. Wonders even you only ever guessed at.

Maybe we'll travel back through the vast rolling fields of space-time as the first galaxies blaze in the wake of the Big Bang. In the endless recycling of the universe, every bit of energy was once part of something else, and we will be too. What will we become?

A hot rock blasting through space in the early days of the universe? One that crashes to Earth and holds the metal that will make the bullet that begins a world war . . . or the bomb that ends another?

Or will that rock become sand, ground by the elements over a million years, then melt in a furnace to make the glass of a telescope that lets curious eyes watch the ancient light of the stars?

Maybe we'll plunge into the primeval swamps and be the energy of the plants that will rot in the earth and become the coal, in a far distant future, that fires a whole civilisation. We might be the lightning bolt that ignites a tree, and gives a young cavewoman and her baby enough warmth to survive – then sparks in her a wondering about how she might make fire herself...

Or we could be the tree that's pulped into the paper on which someone will work out how to break gravity and reach for the stars – or create the world's first atomic bomb.

One day we might even be human again, you and me. Imagine all our energy crystallised into the first cells of a new baby...and what might that baby do with its time on Earth?

Will we surge through the galaxies to the very edges of the universe? Swirl inside nebulous dust-clouds for a billion lifetimes, waiting for a pair of dwarf stars to find each other and fuse into a brand-new sun in a baby galaxy at the frontier of everything...?

You know the best thing I found out, after all that travelling to the edges of the cosmos and back? That love is the engine of the universe. Love is the energy that makes all the lost and broken fragments find each other so that the world can keep creating itself, on and on, until the end of time.

Like we are, Jamie.

So we wing out on the currents of the cosmos, endless tides of tomorrows and yesterdays. You and me, blissed out, imploding into *us*.

We could be anything next.

GREEN FIELDS

Jonathan Stroud

GREEN FIELDS

Before he entered the room, Frank Fisher checked the contents of his satchel. Yes, everything was still in place: the rows of firecrackers and phosphorus pens; the lighters, water flasks and tape-player; the legal documents in their heat-proof plastic sleeve. All nice and neat and ready, just as they had been the last three times he looked. Even so, he took out a lighter and flicked it on briefly, testing the strength of the flame.

Swinging the satchel under his arm, he tried the Velcro fastening that fixed his rapier to his belt. Good and tight – but not so tight he couldn't instantly pull it free if an attack came. All was as it should be. He had everything he needed to survive.

Frank Fisher opened the door.

*

The layout of the room was typical: it could have been a Standard-Class Room of Passing belonging to any of a dozen sects. The floor was smooth, pale wood, the walls matt white. A vase of lilies sat on a reproduction-marble plinth. Several plastic chairs had been arranged beneath the window.

The bed stood alone in the middle of the floor. Until recently it had evidently been surrounded by all the usual medical and devotional aids; the saline drips and heart monitors, the prayer-poles and little bureaux piled with route maps of the Other Side. Now, however, in preparation for the final moments, most of these had been wheeled away to cluster like grieving relatives a short distance from the bed.

Beyond the window, in the high air, seagulls soared. Pale winter light glinted on the cranes and dockyards across the river. The curtains had not been drawn.

Two men stood facing the window, looking up towards the sky. As Frank closed the door, they turned to meet him.

Frank said briskly: 'Frank Fisher, Thirteenth Hour Insurance Company. I guess you'll want to see my accreditation.'

The shorter of the two men nodded to his companion – a thin, pale-faced youth with sparse blond hair. 'Take a look, Benny.'

Benny came forward and unsmilingly examined

the laminate card that Frank held out. Like all employees of the House, he wore a bright-green jacket; in his case, it was just a little too large. The House logo was emblazoned on the lapels, and repeated in a decorative pattern on his tie. His skin was very white. Frank smelled incense hanging round him like a cloud.

The youth's gaze lifted from the card and slid accusingly across Frank's face without meeting his eyes. It dropped away again. 'All seems OK.'

'All right,' the short man said heartily. 'Thanks, Benny. And thank you for coming, Mr Fisher. You've made good time.'

With a roll of his shoulders he stepped forward to shake Frank's hand. Physically he reminded Frank of a cartoon dog from the old shows that ran on the secular entertainment channel – squat and top-heavy, with a broad, powerful torso and spindly legs that tapered fast to tiny patent-leather shoes. His emerald jacket was even brighter than Benny's, and decorated with gold brocade. His voice, his movements, his fine-cut clothes all exuded the same robust, almost brutal, confidence. He said, 'I'm Jeremiah Venal, Manager of the Green Fields House of Passing. As you know, this House is affiliated to the Sacred Brethren whose One Way Forward is the only true path.'

'Amen,' Benny said.

'Can I ask you, Mr Fisher,' Jeremiah Venal said, eyes winking like wet currants above the broadness of his smile, 'to what sect or chapter do you personally belong?'

Frank ran his fingers through his hair, where sweat was already beading. Thanks to the fur lining of his coat, the room's warmth discomfited him. Once, in the early days, he'd worn a long leather mac, which had been black and thin and cooler in every sense. Frank had far preferred it. Unfortunately it had been unsuited to the conditions Beyond, and he had nearly died. 'I'm presently unconnected to any official church,' he said. 'That's the way it has to be, I guess, if I'm to work independently like this.' He moved towards the bed. 'This is Mary Alice Evans? Looks like we haven't got long. I'll need to move all this prayer stuff further out of the way.'

'If you're not a priest,' the blond youth growled, 'you shouldn't be allowed to use your Talent. How can you even think to cross—?'

'That'll do, Benny,' Jeremiah Venal said. 'Mr Fisher, this is, as you say, Mary Alice Evans, age ninety-seven and soon to pass over onto the next stage of her Journey. At such a time the manifold blessings of life boil rapidly away and we're left with two melancholy facts: her body is failing, and she hasn't paid a cent of spiritual insurance to an official sect for thirty-two long years. Not a cent. That being so, we can do nothing further for her.'

The woman's shape showed as a low, bony ridge under the cotton blankets. She was lying on her back, quite still, except where the chest region fluttered with the rapid quiver of her breathing. Only her head and neck were visible, jutting from beneath the sheets like a dead, dry spur of driftwood. The eyes were closed, the toothless mouth gaped blackly. Spread across the pillows was a fan of bone-white hair.

'Poor old girl,' Frank said.

Jeremiah Venal made a clicking noise with his tongue. 'Here at Green Fields we strongly disapprove of anyone who is so cavalier with their preparations for the Other Side. Nevertheless, out of love and charity, we occasionally allow unfortunates who are not insured to pass their final hours with us. And, since we respect the principles of the Free Market, independent practitioners such as you *are* permitted access during the crossing. But in return we *do* expect an appropriate fee.'

Frank was watching the movement of the sheets. Her breaths were very uneven; sometimes loud and ragged, sometimes almost gone. 'Don't worry,' he said, swinging a desk of icons towards the wall, 'you'll get your cut. Twenty per cent. Standard.'

'I mean up front,' Jeremiah Venal said. 'You may come back with nothing.'

Frank looked at him. 'How much up front?'

'Five hundred pounds.'

Frank sucked in his cheeks. 'As you say, I may come back with nothing.'

Jeremiah Venal's smile broadened. 'If you're not happy, you can always leave. I called Floyd Winklebaum as well. You were faster, but he'll be in the foyer downstairs. He'd be delighted to step up and take your place.'

Frank sighed. 'No need. I'm happy.' He produced a crumpled wedge of notes and counted out the total. 'Now, I'll need some space. It's going to be soon.'

Jeremiah Venal folded the money and put it in his jacket pocket. 'Good, good. You do what you have to do. I'll leave you in Benny's capable hands.'

He departed, closing the door loudly. In the centre of the pillow, the dying woman's head jerked; she made an incomprehensible sound.

Frank went on a hasty circuit of the bed, wheeling the medical equipment further off, dragging the bureaux where they'd be safely out of range when the crucial moment came.

'Careful with those,' the blond boy warned.

'Got to be done,' Frank said. 'Wouldn't want me to trample your sacred road maps, would we?'

There was a silence. Frank finished clearing the necessary circle. He pulled a chair over from the window and placed it six feet from the head end of the bed, side on to the woman. Then he switched on a single lamp, drew it closer so that the perimeter of its light fell in an arc across the bed, and closed the curtains. He sat heavily in the chair, sweat dripping from his brow. The tip of his rapier scraped against the floor.

'I don't like your tone,' the youth said.

Frank ignored him. He was looking at the woman now; at the thin, dry arch of her neck, the skull lying heavy on the pillow. She was a thing of wax and bones, and the flame inside her was almost free. He noticed a stain at the corner of the gaping mouth, where someone at some time had tried giving her a nutrition drink. It was an old stain and the drink was long gone. He glanced around. Nor was there a glass of water anywhere. Goddamn Houses of Passing. They were all the same. Now she was going, they couldn't care less.

Of course, it was true that in a little while things like thirst, pain and the disabilities of age would fall away from her like dropped cloth, and wouldn't matter any more. But even so...

Frank fixed his eyes on the woman and tried to clear his mind, get his body ready for the transition. But all he could think about was the parched and open mouth. It distracted him, he couldn't concentrate. 'I think she needs some water,' he said.

The blond youth had settled himself on a chair beside the window, and was peering out through a crack in the curtains. His voice was slightly muffled by the fabric. 'What's it like for you, then?' he said. 'On the Other Side. I've always wondered.'

'You'll see,' Frank said. 'One day.'

'Oh, I know what it'll be like for *me*,' the youth went on. 'I read the Brethren's guidebooks, don't I? I know all about the One True Way. I've memorised the path that'll lead me straight through the Halls to those sweet green pastures. I mean, what's it like *alive*? Going over, getting glimpses. What's it like for you?'

'Lonely,' Frank said shortly. 'Dangerous.' He looked at the ravaged figure in the bed. 'And necessary... Listen, she needs some water. Could you get some, please?'

'Won't be lonely or dangerous for me,' the youth said. 'I've been making regular payments to the Brethren all my life. *I'll* be all right. If I live long enough to get Gold Standard cover, I'll even have an escort. Music. Trumpets. Joyous Psalms being sung as I start to cross the Bridge. Only the truly blessed get all that. Yeah. I'm sorted. But some people don't think ahead, do they? My view is, they've only got themselves to blame.'

Frank was well versed in the patterns of approaching death; he had noticed a subtle change in the rhythm of the woman's breathing. 'Shut up,' he said. 'Go get her some water.'

The youth's voice altered. 'What did you say? You can't speak to me like that. Who do you think you are? I'll call Mr Venal, get you thrown out.'

'If you want him to lose his percentage,' Frank said, 'you go right ahead.' He sighed and stood up abruptly. Opening the flap of his satchel, he took out a flask. 'Don't bother yourself, Benny,' he said. 'You just sit tight. I'll see to it.'

Flicking the spout, he bent at the bedside, put his hand beneath her head. The hair was colourless like threads of glass, and so light he thought it might fall away between his fingers, but the skull was a deadweight in his hand. He lifted her a little and eased a few drops of water onto her dry, grey tongue. The jaw moved; eyes shifted beneath translucent lids. The water ran back into the mouth. She couldn't swallow, but it was cool and pleasant for her, maybe. Frank gave her another few drops, waited to see she didn't choke, then lowered her head down.

'You oughtn't go near anyone who's ready to pass over,' the blond boy hissed. 'That's regulations. You could delay them, block their way.' He spoke softly, but there was something like hatred in his voice. 'Christ, an unbeliever like you. I ought to turf you out myself.' He got up from his chair.

Frank said easily, 'If you lay a hand on me,

I'll knock you through the wall.' He stowed the flask, sat down again, took a deep breath.

'You wouldn't,' the blond boy said. 'You're full of it. You're not a priest. I don't believe people like you go over at all. I hope an abandoned one gets you. I hope you lose your way. I hope you get lost on the endless stairs.'

He kept on talking, but Frank had already tuned him out. He sat very still now. He heard nothing save the faltering rhythm of the woman's breathing, saw nothing save her body on the bed and the way the lamplight fell on the sheets and pillow. When it happened, it would be very quick and subtle; he couldn't afford to miss it. He felt the familiar expectation beating against his heart, sudden and eager and full of fear.

She was stronger than he thought. She hung on for a long time. The day beyond the curtains waned, and the margins of the room had become a deep grey-blue when the lamplight on the bedclothes finally gave its tell-tale quiver. Close beside the bed something happened to the air. Frank saw a pale radiance break through, a narrow rectangular glimmer that shone on nothing. At once Mary Alice Evans sat up, peeled herself free of her mortal body; she swung her legs round and stood suddenly with her head tilted towards the light. She was very faint; even with his Talent, Frank could barely see her. For a moment she paused as if in doubt, her posture hunched and twisted. The limitations of age had been left behind, but its hesitancy could not be instantly unlearned.

Still, she wasn't going to hang around. Frank Fisher had to act fast or she'd be gone.

He rose now and ran with the rapid silence of his Talent, his movement so soft and insubstantial that the youth slumped beside the window noticed nothing. In three strides Frank was at the bed; he reached the woman precisely as she began to walk towards the rectangle of light. Seamlessly, without breaking pace, he turned and followed. She sprang forward. He launched himself after her.

He stayed right behind Mary Alice Evans as she walked out of the world.

Somewhere in the streets below the Green Fields House of Passing came a yelp of drunken laughter. In the shadows of the curtains the blond youth yawned and scratched the back of his neck. The radiance was gone. Frank Fisher was gone. The woman's body lay like snakeskin, discarded in the centre of the bed.

No matter how Frank tried, he could never keep from closing his eyes. He never actually *saw* the moment of transition. So it was always the sharp drop in temperature that he experienced first – and only afterwards, as he forced himself to look, the familiar half-light of the Other Side.

To begin with, as always, his surroundings were nothing but a blur of muted colours, slowly moving, ever-changing. Presently, as always, they resolved themselves into solidity, and he found himself walking behind the woman in the great vistas of the Halls.

They were at a crossroad set between walls of broken brick, which here and there rose vertically to jagged points like teeth or ruined towers. Four paths led away from them. Other paths ran beyond the walls, connected at intervals by arches, gaps and flights of stairs. The ground was thick with red-grey dust, and covered with crisscross lines of footprints, layer upon layer, winding off in all directions through the soft, dark silence.

Frank shivered; even in his coat the air was very cold.

In some places, he knew, the maze entered covered regions, where passages diverged and reconnected under miles of arched brick ceiling. Here, however, there was no such shelter from what was above them.

Raising his eyes despite himself, Frank glimpsed the familiar impossible perspectives, saw the ground on which he stood curl upwards and away forever as if fixed to the inside of some monstrous sphere. Steadily, at first, it rose, with all its spreading paths and routes exposed upon it like a net of veins, then steeper, ever steeper until, at last, faint almost beyond perception, it disappeared cliff-like into the dimness. In places irregular buttresses projected out horizontally above the appalling drop; on some of these were staircases, and minute figures in white walking slowly on them, climbing or descending, lost in their individual journeys through the Halls. And now, as Frank's eyes adjusted properly, he saw that all across the maze, up and down the endless slope, countless other flecks of white were moving – innumerable souls in transit, hunting for escape. Most were alone; a few – Frank could tell by the glints of colour – were accompanied by living priests in capes of gold or green.

As always in such moments, Frank's wits threatened to desert him. Hastily he shook himself free, forcing his mind back to small, controllable things. He tore a phosphorus pen from its holder within the satchel and made his first mark on the nearest flank of wall. The symbol gleamed on the brickwork, fixing his point of entry. Its familiar brightness reassured him. He had his Talent, his equipment and his experience – there was nothing else to fear! Time to get to work, do what he'd come to do. Gripping the hilt of his rapier tightly, he set off after Mary Alice Evans.

She was walking away from him along a path between the walls, her outline framed in the cool half-light. Already her posture had altered: the back was straighter, the hair perhaps a little darker. She moved with increasing speed.

Her bare feet left the faintest prints on the dusty ground. Frank's trainers delved deep furrows as he drew alongside.

Frank cleared his throat. 'Excuse me, Ms Evans?'

He had spoken softly, but even so his voice sounded harsh in the utter quiet. He cast a swift glance at the walls on either side. It would be rare for an abandoned one to find them so quickly, but certainly not impossible. 'Ms Evans?' he said again.

'Yes?' This time she noticed; she broke free of her reverie and turned to face him.

It always took him aback, always surprised Frank what those first moments would do. Particularly with the old ones: how the worn-out surface was transformed, how the built-up sediment of life's experience just dissolved away, leaving the person new. You started following an old woman and ended talking to a girl. It was disconcerting. The long nose was recognisably the same; everything else – the black hair in tresses, the full, wry lips, dark olive eyes, the clear, wide oval of her face – bore no resemblance to the body in the bed. She was taller than him and flushed with youth. Frank felt rather tired.

She said: 'You're not a priest, I hope? I didn't want a priest.'

Frank smiled winningly. 'I'm not a priest, Ms Evans. May I talk with you?'

Her gaze had flitted away from him; she was staring at the arching vaults above. Her face showed no terror, rather a quiet equanimity. 'I suppose . . .'

'Ms Evans, I'm grateful for your time. My name is Frank Fisher. I'm from the Thirteenth Hour Insurance Company. We noticed that at the time of your death you hadn't paid your dues to any accredited spiritual organisation for many years. This means that you are alone and, shall we say, rudderless at what must be a very anxious time. But don't worry, because it doesn't have to be that way. I'm delighted to announce that I can offer you . . .' His voice trailed off. She wasn't listening; she was back to staring at the voids above them. Probably hadn't heard a word he'd said.

Music might do it. That often worked. Cut through their self absorption.

Frank opened his satchel, pressed the button on the tape player. Instantly a tinny music-hall theme sounded, accompanied by jaunty lyrics.

It's not too late for guidance, it's not too late for cheer,
It's not too late, though you've passed through the gate,
Salvation still is near.
Ohhhh, take a little moment to adjust your bearing,
Though you're dead there's no need for swearing,

We're full of love and we're full of caring,
Thirteenth Hour is here.
Ohhhh, take a little look—

'Will you turn that racket off?' the girl said.

Frank switched off the player. Instantly the vast silence swallowed them.

'Jesus,' the girl said. 'I just *died*, and you play me that. What do you want?'

Frank spoke in a hurt voice. 'The Thirteenth Hour theme tune provides comfort to many wandering souls.'

'Not me,' the girl said. 'It gives me a headache.'

She was a feisty one; clearly it was going to be difficult. Frank sighed inwardly. He thought of the five hundred pounds he'd paid to get this far.

'Just a couple of words, Ms Evans,' he said. 'Maybe you don't realise it, but you're in a very vulnerable post-death position. See, as I said before, you're not covered by any spiritual insurance.'

The girl blew out her cheeks. 'I guess I let it slide. I must've forgotten.'

Frank said, 'You let your payments to the Way Made Manifest sect lapse thirty-two years ago, Ms Evans, and you've not taken up with anyone else. This "forgetfulness" means you've arrived here without help of any kind.'

She smiled then. 'That's all right. I'm OK.'

Frank shook his head. 'You're still acclimatising. I understand you might be a little confused.' He made a little rueful gesture at the ruined landscape. 'Look around you and consider. It's happened. You're here in the Halls. Now there's a long journey ahead if you're to ever reach the sweet Green Fields. It's a journey full of perils, Ms Evans, as I'm sure you know. Pits, labyrinths and wastes – and the abandoned ones hunting those who give up hope. And you've arrived without any guides, maps, relics or defences.'

'Yes, that was by choice,' the girl said. 'I didn't *want* a priest. Now, if you're—'

'Oh sure, the priests can't do everything they say,' Frank said. 'They don't know the One True Way. They can't get you all the way to the Bridge and Journey's End. No one can. But they *can* escort you for a while, get you used to the dangers, ward off pursuit.'

He glanced behind him instinctively, saw no shadows moving against the walls. 'I can do that too,' he said. 'I'm an experienced operator.' He tapped his rapier. 'And I'm armed.'

The girl was looking at him with new attention. 'Have I met you before?' she said. 'I recognise your voice...'

'I was in the room,' Frank said. 'When you passed over. That's how I'm with you now.'

The girl shrugged. 'What precisely are you offering me, Mr... er, Fisher?'

'Thirteenth Hour believe your lack of cover is due to honest oversight on your part,' Frank said, 'probably caused by senility on account of your advanced age. Don't feel bad – it happens to many people. But it's not too late. You're dead, but I can accompany you for a while.'

'No thanks,' the girl said. 'I'm content as I am, and I have no means of paying you. I appreciate the offer. Now, goodbye.' With a gentle smile, she walked away to where two other paths diverged through arches in the walls. Without hesitation she took the left-hand way. Frank cursed under his breath. With his phosphorus pen he drew a hasty sign at the junction to mark his route and hurried after her.

The path descended down a flight of steps with high walls pressing on either side. The light there was muted; it was just the sort of place, Frank felt, where abandoned ones might lurk. He loosened the Velcro strapping at his belt. 'Ms Evans, wait! You're making a mistake. You *can* pay me – all you have to do is sign this paper here!'

This time, when she turned, her smile was gone. 'I beg your pardon?'

Frank drew level, panting; the air on the Other Side was poor. He rummaged in his satchel, drew out the documents in their plastic folder. 'It seems you left one hundred thousand pounds in the bank,' he said. 'One hundred thousand pounds with no one to claim it. No family, no heirs. That fact buys you a lifeline, Ms Evans. If you sign this contract, bequeathing the full amount posthumously to Thirteenth Hour Insurance, I personally will give you immediate and invaluable assistance. I will escort you through this desolation as far as I can, warding off all dangers, guiding you until you're able to fend for yourself.' He took a deep breath, scanning the impassive face for clues. 'Think about it. You'll have a much better chance of ultimately reaching the Fields if I'm here to start you off. And all that money doesn't go to waste. Makes sense, doesn't it?' He smiled at her. 'What do you say?'

'I say…' The girl folded her arms. 'I say you've got a bloody cheek.'

Frank hesitated. 'Perhaps if I explained again—'

'No! Not another word! You followed me here trying to *sell* me something? You followed me *here*? You're worse than the priests!' Her dark eyes shone in the half-light; perhaps it was her anger, but her face seemed more beautiful than before. 'At least *they* give up hounding you when you die. *Selling* me something! And in *this* place…'

'But that's the point,' Frank began. 'This place is—'

She was off again, hurrying away without a backward glance. Likewise she utterly ignored the holes and crevices in the walls on either side. Frank shook his head as he hurried after her. She was just the sort the abandoned ones liked; confused, proud and careless, drifting without purpose. Noisy too. He drew his rapier, and arranged his satchel so that his lighter and firecrackers were at his fingertips.

'Ms Evans—'

'Long ago,' the girl said, stopping so suddenly he almost bumped into her, 'I grew sick of people selling me assurances to use after death. Offering me road maps, teaching me songs to sing to guarantee safe passage – always contradicting each other, always swearing *they* knew the One True Path. You know what I realised, Mr Fisher? At its heart, it's all about the money. And you've just proved it.'

It seemed to Frank that while she spoke he heard something, a little noise from elsewhere, half-hidden by her words. Scratching, shuffling? Hard to be sure, she was speaking so loudly. He stepped across to stand between her and the nearest wall, where a narrow fissure split the bricks in two. The cleft was dark and probably too tight for anything to squeeze through, but he kept it in the corner of his vision. 'No,' he said doggedly, 'that's not right. At least not always. Me being here is about your safety. It's about me helping you to—'

'I don't *need* your help,' the girl said. 'Surely that's perfectly obvious. I'm safe here. Now go away.'

'Think carefully, Ms Evans. You're making a hasty decision—'

'Too right I am.'

'And it's a foolish one! You don't know what you're doing. Look around you—'

'No, Mr Fisher. *You* look around!' She raised her voice again; reverberations ran through the nearest bricks and away across the Halls. 'Look around and tell me – what precisely is it that you fear?'

She glared at him: for a moment their eyes met. Then his gaze slid away, up and out across the infinite, curving vastness, where countless souls moved ant-like in their separate journeys... For a moment the terrible solitariness of existence on the Other Side pressed down upon him. He felt crushed by its weight, by its remorseless scale and silence. His head spun; he could hardly breathe.

In a small voice he said, 'As well as guidance and protection, I'm offering temporary companionship after death. That's no small thing. That's what I'd want if it were me.'

When he looked again, the anger in her eyes had quieted a little. She said softly: 'I quite understand. Thank you for the offer, Mr Fisher, but it's not necessary for me.'

Frank's shoulders slumped a little. 'OK,' he said. 'OK.' Closing his satchel, he fixed his rapier to his belt and wiped a hand across his brow. Despite the cold, his face felt flushed. Five hundred pounds gone and nothing to show for it. But what could you do? You just couldn't tell; a person's character was a mystery until you got them on the Other Side. Some people wept at his feet, some thanked him like a brother. Mary Alice Evans told him to get lost. So it went. He reached for his water bottle, flicked up the spout and took a long drink. And now what? Just the pain of the journey home. Each time he stepped back, he felt worse afterwards. Like it was taking something out of him.

He stowed the bottle and turned to go. 'I'm sorry to have bothered you,' he said.

To his surprise the girl hadn't yet moved; she stood there, watching him.

'Back in the room,' she said, 'just before I died. Didn't you—?'

As she spoke, soft sounds came from the crevice by Frank's side. Even as he heard them, he knew he had been careless. Disappointment had made him drop his guard.

He threw himself backwards, landing awkwardly on one buttock in a cloud of dust, and thus narrowly avoiding the clasp of a hand that extended from the darkness of the cleft. It was a white hand that hung on the end of a long white arm; swiping vainly in midair, it dropped swiftly to the dust where it walked, questing on its fingers in little jerks and rushes like a spider, closer and closer to Frank's outstretched leg. Frank gave a squeal, wrenched his rapier clear of his belt and, with an oath, brought it down onto the centre of the pale, thin wrist. Bone snapped in two; the arm jerked back. The severed hand lay on the ground, its fingers curling, flexing. Still sitting on his bottom in the dust, Frank snared it with the tip of his rapier and flicked it quickly upwards and away into the darkness of the cleft.

Somewhere close by came an angry gnashing of teeth. A shadow moved beyond the bricks. Frank dropped the rapier, got to his feet, took his lighter and a firecracker from his bag. He lit the firecracker and, with a practised movement, threw it into the hole. There was a flash of phosphorus and a plaintive wailing. Then there was silence. Frank stood with another firecracker ready, eyes scanning the walls around. Nothing moved.

Presently he relaxed. The usual sense of grim exultation surged in him. He picked up his rapier and wiped the tip through the thick grey dust.

'Mr Fisher.'

The girl was standing as before, gazing at him without expression.

'Pass me the paper,' she said. 'I've changed my mind. I'll sign the contract, give you the money.'

Well, it was only natural after what had happened. 'You've made a wise choice to stick with me,'

Frank said, wiping his brow. 'Just let me find my pen.'

He located the biro in its neat compartment. Mary Alice Evans took it and wrote her signature at the bottom of the paper. Her style was slightly ornate and fussy: an old woman's hand.

She put the top on the pen and handed it back. 'There. Will that do?'

Frank nodded. 'Perfect. It'll stand up nicely in a court of law.'

'That's fine,' she said. 'Well, goodbye.'

Frank Fisher stared at her. 'What do you mean? Don't you understand? I'm coming with you.'

'No, you're not,' the girl said. 'I never agreed to that. I just said I'd give you the money. That's what you wanted, isn't it?'

He frowned. 'Yes, but . . . clearly you need my protection.'

When she smiled she looked younger than ever, practically a child. 'That's not why I signed your precious bit of paper, Mr Fisher. I signed because I suddenly remembered what you did for me.'

There was a pause. Frank said, 'You mean just now? When the abandoned—'

'No. You gave me a drink, don't *you* remember? Back in the last place. You cradled my head and gave me water. You gave me comfort. For *that* I'm giving you the money. And now I'm going on – alone.'

It seemed to Frank that he was missing something. The side of his skull ached. He rubbed his hand across his temple. 'Well, of course,' he said, 'I remember. But that was just a little thing, and I'm talking about the dangers facing you *now*. The abandoned ones are on your scent already. They follow anyone who's lost, who's drifting without purpose. They've already attacked you.'

'No, Mr Fisher, they attacked *you*.' The girl's smile broadened. 'I didn't see them.'

'*What*? But it was right there!' He waved his hand behind him at the wall.

'Maybe for you.' There was laughter in her eyes: it angered and confused him all at once. 'It wasn't real for me,' she said. 'I didn't see any monsters. I just saw you yelling and waving your sword about – after falling on your backside in the grass.'

'You must have seen it!' Frank said. 'I know it happened fast, but—' He hesitated. It had taken a moment for the meaning of the word to get through to him. 'Grass?' he said.

'We're standing in it now.' Mary Alice Evans gestured all around. 'Do you not see it, Mr Fisher? Don't you feel it beneath your feet?'

He found himself staring stupidly down at the dust and stones of the arid ground. 'Of course not. What do you mean? There's no grass among the walls.'

'Maybe,' the girl said. 'But then, I can't see the walls, either.'

She was looking past him at something, her eyes glistening with reflected light.

Almost eagerly, Frank followed her gaze – but all he saw was the barren labyrinth rising endlessly ahead. He looked away.

'Oh dear,' the girl said. 'I'm sorry for you. Perhaps it does mean something to be dead after all.'

Frank said, 'But . . . but we're in the Halls, Ms Evans. Everyone starts—'

'Everyone's different, Mr Fisher. For me it's been the Green Fields since the moment I died.' Her smile now was very beautiful; its radiance wounded him. 'And I'm looking forward to my journey through them, however long it takes. Goodbye, Mr Fisher. Thank you again for being so kind to me. I hope someone someday does the same for you.'

She waved, and walked away along the path. Presently she came to a junction, turned aside and was gone. Frank Fisher gazed after her, the contract hanging limply in his hand. Then he spun steadily on his heels, looking round him at the tight brick walls that sealed him in, at the infinite tracts of pathways up above.

He closed his eyes . . . and quickly opened them. Did he see a flash of green?

No. He couldn't say he did.

Frank Fisher took a long, deep breath. He stowed the documents and pen carefully back in his satchel. He checked the firecrackers and phosphorus pens. He tried the compartments... Yes, everything nice and neat, ready for when he needed them again.

Closing the flap, he drew himself up and, with his hand on the hilt of his rapier, began slowly to retrace his painful way back to the mortal world.

'THESE ARE THE YOLKS, FOLKS!'

Philip Ardagh

'THESE ARE THE YOLKS, FOLKS!'

'If you have to praise God to get into heaven then you'd better be sure you're praising the *right* God, because – if you're praising the *wrong* one – you could be making things a lot worse for yourself,' my little sister said to me when she was about nine and going through her Religious Knowledge phase.

'Uhu,' I said, nodding my head cautiously. I wasn't sure where, if anywhere, this conversation was going.

'So I reckon it's better not to praise *any* God. That way, if he's a forgiving God he might forgive you for not praising him, and if he's a vengeful God there isn't much you can do about it anyway. And, at least, you haven't taken the wrong side and made him even *more* angry.'

Vengeful? Now there was a big word for a small girl. 'Eat your supper,' I said, 'Mum will be back soon.'

I plonked the plate of food in front of her. I'd tried to arrange it to look like a Muppet's face, more for my own satisfaction than hers. I liked to express my artistic side and love-of-Muppets through food sculpting. I'd put her orange juice in a Muppet glass. It had a picture of Rowlf, the piano-playing dog, on both sides. I don't think Claudia – that's my sister's name – thought it was babyish. She's used to it. My 'Muppetmania' she calls it. It's something I got off Mum, along with my brown hair.

Another time, Claudia suddenly came out with: 'Dan, if God the Father, God the Son and God the Holy Ghost are all one and the same, like the Reverend Morris says they are, then how come Jesus was calling out to God when he was on the cross? Was he just talking to himself like that crazy woman we see at the bus stop?'

I felt I had something to contribute to this particular debate and, anyway, I didn't have any food to distract her with. 'Crazy Anna at the bus stop isn't talking to herself, Claudia,' I told her. 'She's talking on a hands-free mobile.'

'Then why's she called Crazy Anna?'

'Because she lives with a man in a carrot suit,' I explained. (Which was true, though he didn't wear it all day, every day. Having said that, I did once see him in it – frayed foliage, cigarette burns and all – when he was down at the Jobcentre Plus. He wore it with point upwards, foliage like a kilt. It was impressive in its own, seen-better-days, *weird* kind of way. There's something disturbing about watching a giant carrot smoke, but I can't quite put my finger on exactly what that is.)

'But if he's the one in the carrot suit, why isn't *he* called Crazy Whatever-His-Name-Is?'

'Because nobody seems to *know* his name,' I said.

'I expect Crazy Anna does,' said Claudia.

I had to agree. I expect Crazy Anna, of all people, did.

(In the Muppets there's a guy called Crazy *Harry*. He's the one with the detonator – the box with the plunge-down handle, shaped like the letter T – who's always blowing up stuff. He has an anarchist's beard. It never even occurred to me what an anarchist's beard was until, one day, I was looking at a load of pictures of a group of anarchists, and just about all the men had beards just like Crazy Harry's.)

Other questions from Claudia of a religious nature included:

'If Judas hadn't done what he'd done, then Jesus couldn't have come back from the dead, could he? Unless someone else went and betrayed him. So Judas must have done what God *wanted* him to do, so he can't really have been bad then, can he? Like Mother Theresa, Judas was just following God's orders. What's it called?'

This was asked, without so much as a pause for breath, when she was climbing onto one of those wiz-along pulleys at the adventure playground where everything is made out of old telegraph poles, and the ground is ankle-deep in soggy brown woodchip.

'God's bidding? God's will?' I suggested. 'Is that what you mean?'

'That's it.' My little sister nodded. 'And everyone thinks Mother Theresa was great. Except for Minnie Thompson, but she has a thing against nuns, even ones with very wrinkly faces.'

Claudia disappeared along the pulley with a '*Weeeeeeeeeeeeeeeee!*'

Minnie Thompson was the very old lady who used to live in the flat below ours in Albermare Street. She had been born a Jew but saved from the Nazis by a Christian couple who pretended she was their own daughter, and brought her up a Christian. Minnie thought this was wrong. She thought that they should have secretly brought her up as a Jew, and she still complained about it over sixty years later. Mum thought this was ungrateful (though she never said so to Minnie's face). But Brian, my stepdad, said he could understand Minnie's point of view, especially when you considered that Minnie's real parents were gassed in a concentration camp for their beliefs. 'No wonder she feels that being Jewish is important,' he said. 'It defines her whole life.'

And then there was the time Claudia said, 'Dan?'

And I said, 'Yes?'

And she said, 'If Jesus hadn't been crucified but had been run over by a donkey and cart, would Christians wear little gold donkeys and carts on chains around their necks, and would there be little models of donkeys and carts on church altars?'

And I told her that a very wise man called Lenny Bruce once said that if Jesus had been executed nowadays, it would probably have been in the electric chair, and Christians would probably wear little electric chairs instead of crosses.

So Claudia scuttled off the sofa and Googled *Lenny+Bruce* on the family computer in the kitchen – where Mum could make sure she wasn't being groomed by online paedophiles masquerading as cute kittens in baskets – and came back spouting a string of swear words.

Mum was not impressed and, for some reason, it was all my fault.

'I thought the computer was supposed to have some nanny-type-filter thingy on it,' I said.

'Brian deactivated it when Claudia wanted to check out something about the Earl of Essex for homework,' said Mum.

'Huh?'

'The word "Essex" has the word "sex" in it, so the filter wouldn't let her Google it,' she explained.

A likely story. Anyhow, didn't that make it *Brian's* fault, not mine? Apparently not.

By the time she got around to asking me about the small matter of Christ in the tomb, Claudia was going through her 'improving the Bible' phase. (She'd already suggested a subtle addition to Genesis, adding a line about Noah leaving behind the dinosaurs in the Great Flood. When I'd said, 'But what about the unicorns?' she'd looked at me like I was an idiot. 'There's no such thing,' she'd said. She was taking this stuff *seriously*.)

'I don't get it,' said Claudia one day, when I was trying to find the puncture in the back tyre of my bike by sticking the inner tube in a washing-up bowl of water and looking out for little bubbles. 'Get what about what?' I asked.

'The big deal about Jesus's tomb being open and him gone. That could just mean someone broke in and took the body. Where's the mystery in that? If we came home and found the front door wide open and Goldie missing' – Goldie is her goldfish – 'then we'd guess someone broke in and took her...'

'So?'

'Wouldn't it have been more of a miracle if Jesus had been spotted in the garden, so they broke the seal, rolled away the stone and *then* found his body gone . . . the tomb empty?'

'Like one of those locked-room mysteries Gran likes to read?' I asked.

'Exactly!' said Claudia, triumphantly.

Gran used to read these very old paperback books published by a company called Penguin, which is still going. Their books have been around for years, and these were really, really old ones where the type inside was tiny. (No one in their right mind would print a book with type that small nowadays.) The paper was so old that the pages were browning at the edges. And all the covers looked the same, except for the book titles. There were no pictures or anything, just a strip of green along the top and along the bottom and a penguin logo (which wasn't always the same). Her favourite locked-room-mystery authors were Carter Dickson and John Dickson Carr. I say authors, *plural*, but one day I Googled them and found out that they were, in fact, one and the same person . . . so Gran's favourite authors turned out to be just one author, which felt a bit like having solved a mystery myself. (Not that I knew it was one until I'd solved it, if you see what I mean.)

'But just because your version of Jesus's tomb still being sealed shut would make a better story, doesn't mean that's how it happened—' I began.

'How it happened *if* the Bible's true,' my little sister corrected me.

'If the Bible's true.' I nodded.

You'll have guessed by now that we come from a Christian household. Not Christian as in going-to-church Christian. No, not that. I don't think Mum and Brian have ever been to church, except for a few of my cousin's weddings. (One cousin, three weddings.) Dad's funeral was at a crematorium, and Mum and Brian didn't even get married in church. They got married in a register office which looked like a fire station. (I thought they were called 'registry offices' with a 'y' on the end, but this one certainly wasn't.) Neither Claudia nor I is christened, and Mum and Brian don't even go to a church carol service at Christmas, just the ones at the school hall.

I mean we're Christians as in we're not-Jewish-or-Muslim-or-Sikh or anything else like that.

One Christmas, Claudia and I wrote a song called 'I'm Only a Christian Because of the Food' and performed it on Boxing Day. I wore a T-shirt which looked like a *Beatles* album cover, except John, Paul, George and Ringo's faces had been swapped for Fozzie, Kermit, Gonzo and Animal's (though not necessarily in that order). I played a quarter-size guitar I'd been given when I was about seven, and Claudia sang into the handle of a skipping rope, pretending it was a microphone. She wore a strange woolly hat on her head and imagined it was a glamorous wig.

The lyrics to the chorus went:

'Christmas arrives.
Another year has passed.
Let's get into
The festive mood.
It's time for turkey
And Christmas pud at last.
I'm only a Christian
Because of the food.
Yes, I'm only a Christian
Because of the foooood!'

There were a couple of verses, but they weren't as good – as finely tuned – and referred to our next-door neighbours and friends, who you've never heard of, so there's no point in talking about them here (though I do remember being proud of rhyming 'posh' with 'nosh', which sounded pretty posh in its own right).

We sang it about a gazillion times and then fell about laughing. Mum clearly liked it, and I think Brian (who's Claudia's real dad) did too, though he acted as though he half-thought he shouldn't approve because it might offend someone who wasn't even there. I'm not saying it was genius – we were only young kids – but it was definitely a good laugh. It certainly wasn't lame.

That was the Christmas I was given a book called *The Works* by Jim Henson. Jim Henson was the man who created the Muppets. He was a genius because, as well as being the creator, he was the original Kermit the Frog, and the spirit – the heart – of all the shows. The book was full of brilliant photographs and behind-the-scenes stuff. It became one of my favourite books and, over the years, it not only became dog-eared and well thumbed, but it was also where I kept Muppet-related pictures and articles I'd cut out of newspapers and magazines. There were even flattened chocolate-bar wrappers.

Because I went to a C of E school – which means Church of England, whatever Max Hollis told me on my first day in Reception – we got to do a proper nativity play in Infants (not just one of those Winter Shows they do in some schools where the Baby Jesus doesn't even get a mention, and people dress up as the East Wind and a snowflake and stuff).

I played Joseph, which wasn't the lead but I felt it was pretty cool at the time because I got to wear a false beard stuck on with spirit gum – like professional actors use – and not held in place with a piece of elastic around the head. The gum smelled like nothing else I've ever smelled before or since.

I also got a decent prop: one I actually got to use, rather than just hold, like a shepherd's crook or a shoe box covered in gold wrapping paper (like one third of the three wise men had to carry).

It was a hammer. I was a carpenter, so I got to hammer a piece of wood in my workshop and to say, 'God be with you!' to people passing by. I can't remember why most of them were passing, but I do remember that they were all either wearing tea towels or Woolworth's shepherd's-costume head-dresses on their heads. (Woolworth's doesn't exist any more. Times change.)

I only had the one line in the play, so it was easy to learn but, at the same time, because I got to say it lots of times, it was quite a big speaking part. And it was also cool to be playing the Baby Jesus's dad. Well, stepdad, I suppose. And at least I didn't have to kiss Ginger Norris, who played Mary.

When it came around to Claudia being in Infants, she played the non-speaking part of a lobster.

She wasn't bothered that there weren't lobsters mentioned being in the stable at Bethlehem in the Bible. She appreciated that, if everyone in her year had to get a part, then some of them would have to be sheep or rocks or whatever, and the lobster costume really stood out. No, what bothered my little sister was that the lobster costume was red, 'And lobsters are only red once they've been boiled,' she said. 'And I'm not playing a *dead* lobster.'

Brian came up with a brilliant answer, which I've never forgotten. He said that perhaps the innkeeper-who-had-no-room-at-the-inn felt guilty about putting Mary and Joseph in the stable, so he'd cooked them a nice lobster supper but, because the Baby Jesus was born, it was a magical night and a miracle occurred, and the lobster came back to life. That made Claudia feel *really* special.

For some reason, it reminded me of that old tale of another Christmas miracle and no – surprise, surprise – I'm not about to harp on about *The Muppet Christmas Carol* (which is probably my third favourite Muppet film after *The Great Muppet Caper* and *The Muppets Take Manhattan)*. The miracle I was thinking of was the one that every Christmas Eve farmyard animals are said to be able to talk to each other in a language people will understand. Mum likes to listen to the radio when she's doing a big pile of ironing, and once we both listened to an afternoon story about the farmyard animals, read by the posh bloke in Mum's favourite film, *Four Weddings and a Funeral*, who was also in *The Vicar of Dibley*.

I liked it.

It stuck in my mind for some reason, as did a radio play about this old woman who's obsessed with wanting to own this amber necklace. She was even willing to kill for it. I think liking the story so much had something to do with the faintest memory I had of my real Dad which included him having a keyring with a big, blobby chunk of amber on the end.

'He never did, you know,' said Mum when I asked her about it once. 'I wonder what you're confusing it with? Your memory's playing tricks.'

But the memory was so strong I never let it go. Dad and the chunk of amber. The memory belonged to me. My link with a dad who died when I was around two and a half. I wasn't about to give it up for anyone.

There was a brief period when Claudia's Religious Knowledge enquires strayed beyond Christianity. Reincarnation was the next big thing.

'Buddhas believe that when you die you come back as something else,' she told me, out of the blue one weekend, when we were putting a load of my old bike magazines up in the loft.

'You mean Buddhists,' I said. 'And it's called reincarnation.'

'Transmigration,' said Claudia. And who was I to argue? 'So if you've been good, you come back as a panther or a grizzly bear or something big and strong, but if you've been bad you come back as a beggar or a toad or—'

'A cabbage?' I suggested. I was thinking of those Muppet vegetables-with-faces cowering from the Swedish Chef's kitchen knives. Or chainsaw. Or bazooka.

Claudia shook her head. 'No, not a cabbage. You have to come back as a live thing.'

'Plants are alive,' I reasoned.

'Alive as in an *animal* or *person* kind of alive,' said Claudia. 'Things which think.'

I grunted. I was carrying a very heavy cardboard box up the loft ladder.

'But what I don't get is this,' said my sister.

'What?' I sighed and rested the corner of the box on a rung of the ladder.

'If you don't remember who or what you were before you died and were reborn, you won't feel you're being punished being a toad because you'll only remember being a toad.'

'Oh,' I said. 'Pass me that, will you?' I pointed to a magazine that had dropped onto the landing floor.

Anyway, you get the picture. Religion or faith or belief or whatever you choose to call it wasn't a big deal in our family. Even Claudia grew out of her Religious Knowledge phase and started asking sciency questions, such as, 'Why do dolphins look like they're smiling?' and, 'Does the earth weigh a bit less every time something is blasted off into space?'

I'll let you try and get your head around that last one, if you have the time or the inclination.

Me? I think we should come to the part where I was dying.

Ready? I wasn't. It was a bigger jump than this.

One minute I was dashing into the underpass, pulling my coat around me to keep out the rain. The worse thing I had to worry about was the hole in the bottom of my trainers. Then:

STAB!

And as the knife went in – at that very moment – I heard the words, *These are the yolks, folks!* as clearly as if they were spoken.

My attacker didn't say them.

He was spouting religion, but in a nonsensical way, jumbled up with a load of swear words and madly repeating the word 'sorry'.

'Sorry-sorry-sorry-sorry-sorry.' And he sounded like he really meant it. Unshaven face. Thick, dark stubble. Spit in the corners of his mouth. 'Sorry-sorry-sorry-sorry-sorry.'

Madly repeating it.

Genuinely mad.

Mad and sad. A poor mentally ill man whose pleas for help were ignored by others. *'Help me. I'm going to do something bad. Really bad.'*

But no help came. So he did bad.

That bad was killing me.

These are the yolks, folks!

They're from a DVD. The words. They're from a DVD, not that a DVD was playing. I simply heard them in my head, or all around me. Or somehow both.

It's the Muppets version of Humpty Dumpty singing his cheery song.

You'll find it on YouTube.

It's out there.

These are the yolks, folks! These are the yolks.

I actually managed to smile.

The knife – the stab wound – hurt. Yes. It hurt, but with the words came a real comfort. Thoughts of Mum, Brian, a very young Claudia and me watching Muppet DVDs together. Our family time, shared with a frog, a bear, a pig and a whatever. Kermit, Fozzie, Miss Piggy and Gonzo.

Fozzie with the sad eyes, hat and the waggling ears.

Mum's tales of seeing *The Great Muppet Caper* four – or was it five? – times in the same week in the same cinema, when it was first released back in 1984. The cinema in St Martin's Lane in London, that's now that weird-looking hotel and a gym.

I told you where I got my Muppetmania from, didn't I?

And, do you know what? The Muppets were with me then. They surrounded me. I was enveloped by them. I could smell their synthetic fur.

They were bright. They were cheerful. They were furry and feathery. Bright-coloured and snugly like a blanket. They were the comfort of happy memories.

These are the yolks, folks!

Comfort.

Yes, that's the word.

There was something very *comforting* about being surrounded by Muppets. They were all around me, everywhere. Scooter was looking down on me with his ping-pong-ball eyes.

Kissy, kissy, said Miss Piggy.

I wish you'd married Kermit. I wish Jim Henson hadn't died.

I was crying. I was crying, but not for me. This was crazy. Henson had years – more life – than I'd had, but I was crying for *him*, a man I never knew.

There was Gonzo – The *Great* Gonzo – and his chickens.

Chick-i-babes.

As the warm blood pumped out of me, the pain was still there but less important, somehow. It was no longer a surprise, but a part of me.

These are the yolks, folks!

My breathing was getting harder. Shallower, but more effort. I didn't usually think about breathing... but now every breath was conscious: centre stage.

Breath in. Out. In. Out.

Christ! I was dying.

Christ, I didn't believe in you. All those questions Claudia asked, and I never really believed in you.

But what if...? If...?

Or the God of David? Or Mohammed?

Or Krishna? Was Krishna a god or a prophet... or neither or both?

Christ. I was dying. I needed something…

Was this the end? It couldn't be it. Not when Humpty Dumpty was about to announce that he was to play the lead role in Shakespeare's *Omelette*.

These are the yolks, folks!

And then there was Dr Bunsen Honeydew, with his head like a honeydew melon. No eyes, just glasses…and his hapless assistant, Beaker. It was hard to feel totally alone – totally helpless – with Beaker there.

Mi-mi-mi-mi-mi…

Life was ebbing. I closed my eyes now. All I could see was a blob of light. A blob of colour.

Amber, warm and inviting. And a voice.

*

IS THERE AN AFTERLIFE?
by
Claudia Richards

Is my brother Dan in heaven?

If it's up in the fluffy clouds, I hope not.
He never liked heights.

Is there an afterlife?

Yes. It's the life of those of us he left behind.
We have to get on with LAD: Life After Dan.

Do I think of him often?

Only every single day. His old Kermit the Frog stuffed toy is on my chest of drawers now. He loved the Muppets.

Wouldn't it be great if his heaven was full of them?

Oh yes. Them and his dad. That would be heaven for him.

SURFACE WATER

Gillian Philip

SURFACE WATER

I must be the youngest person on the ship. And I don't want to seem ungrateful or anything, but it's not as if I asked to be here. I'm not even sure why I'm here at all. I have no memory of getting here, but for some reason that's not what's bothering me.

So I'm standing on the aft bit of Deck Seven (I may not like this place much, but at least I'm making an effort with the terminology) in the tight smoker-cluster, where they're all trying to huddle under the jutting roof and keep their fags alight in the drizzle that blows in sideways. I don't smoke, of course, but it's my best chance of staying out of *his* way.

I'm not entirely sure he wants to be in my way, either. But best to be on the safe side.

*

I didn't even know he was on board with me, not to begin with. He didn't even show up in the first day's photo gallery, after the ship stopped at my port. Maybe he got on at a different point.

It turns out the ship has this official photographer, who is like the paparazzi from hell. I don't even remember him being there but he must have got a photo of me as I came on board, because there I am in the row of mug shots, looking furtive. The picture is not very flattering; I'm visibly startled. My woolly hat is pulled down over my forehead and my anorak collar is up and I'm peering out from in between like a surprised hedgehog. Clearly I didn't brush my hair before I put the hat on.

Surreptitiously I edge the photo under the one next to it, so all you can see is my sleeve.

'I don't believe it,' says the woman beside me. She doesn't say it to me but to her husband. 'That's the couple we met on the Greek Islands cruise.' She points at a print I can't see. 'I couldn't stand her.'

He grunts.

'How are we going to avoid them? It's not exactly a big boat. This is absolutely typical. Obviously they let just anyone in.'

He grunts again.

'Look.' She points at another photo. 'He's famous. Something in a movie. In space.'

Marginally more interested, her husband peers through his specs. 'Maybe we'll see him around.'

'I doubt it.' The woman sounds disapproving. 'I expect he's up on the penthouse deck. Cloud Nine. He won't mix with the likes of us.'

She flounces away towards reception as if she's been snubbed by his photo alone, but her dignity takes a knock when she's almost sent flying by a striding girl in a tight black top. The cross woman opens her mouth indignantly, but the girl ignores her. She also ignores the bloke at her heels, who's trying to keep up.

'Sally, listen, I'm sorry—'

'Bit late for that. I told you not to drive so fast. *I told you.*'

Embarrassed, I gaze intently at the gallery till they've disappeared down the corridor, with him still snatching at her sleeve and pleading. The atmosphere on board is not especially nice. No wonder nobody looks happy in these photos.

Some of the people in the pictures are grinning and attempting a wave but mostly they're like me: taken aback, ill at ease. You'd think they were as surprised to be on the damn cruise as I was. One frowny bearded guy has his hand up towards the camera like a defensive celeb leaving a sleazy nightclub.

The photographer himself hovers by the photo gallery, grinning proudly, as we examine his work.

All the staff are so impossibly cheerful and friendly, I feel even grumpier in their presence.

I'm sidling away and thinking I'll escape to my cabin on Deck Five when I hear the whisper.

'MARNIE.'

You're thinking nobody whispers in capital letters, but he can. Everything he ever does, he does in uppercase.

I freeze and my throat constricts and I catch sight of the shadow in the corner of my eye. It's not much more than a movement, but it's there. All the same, when I turn on my heel it's gone.

I know I didn't imagine him.

That's when I decide to go and hide in the smoking zone.

Everybody on Deck Seven seems to smoke. They're all puffing desperately, so much so that I wonder if they're affecting the climate. It's hardly cruising weather anyway. The sea isn't terribly rough but it's a uniform steel-grey flecked with white, and so is the sky. The line between the two is just a foggy blur three hundred and sixty degrees around. I'm already longing for land. Actually, I miss land, with an aching need, and I don't like the way I'm getting used to the slight pitch and roll of the ground beneath my feet.

Down on the stern below there's the pool and Jacuzzi. I said the sea wasn't that choppy, but the pool is overflowing after a rainstorm and it's sloshing with the roll of the ship, flumping out and cascading back in like some outsized water feature. There's a couple swimming in it anyway, gamely fighting the swell, disappearing under the waves for seconds at a time.

'Sooner them than me,' says the woman to my left, taking another drag on her Embassy. She's got a pinched yellow look and a liverish gleam in her eye. 'Anyways, you'd think they'd be averse to water after the – you know. The thing. With the riptide.'

'Well, you'd think we'd be averse to these,' says her pal, tapping her fag.

The first one giggles. 'Well, we beat it, didn't we? In a manner of speaking.'

This time they both giggle. I don't get what's so funny, but hey, I'm confused about everything.

'Give us a smile, kid. Whatcha doing on this deck anyway, if you don't smoke?'

'Ah, leave her alone. She'll be avoiding somebody. So would you be if you'd ended up on Deck Five.'

'*Hmph*. Anyway, I bet the pool on Deck Cloud Nine's a bit calmer than that one,' says Smoker Two, stubbing out her fag and lighting another as she nods at the swimmers.

'Wouldn't know.' Smoker One shrugs. 'You been up there?'

'Can't find the stair.'

'It's a labyrinth, so it is.'

So it certainly is. I wonder if it's got a minotaur; that might be what I'm seeing out of the corner of my eye. That's what I'm thinking, in an ironic half-amused way, when I see it again, a smear of movement.

No, it's not a monster; not one with a bull's head, anyway. It's definitely him. I slink back into the damp shadow of the smoking zone. I don't want him to find me. Not like last time.

Last time isn't exactly crystal clear. It's more of a feeling than a memory. Still, the feeling's surprisingly strong, like a vivid dream you can't quite catch when you wake up.

Last time he found me, I thought I'd done a good job of hiding. Last time, I thought it was going to be OK.

I can't remember if it was or not.

I tell the nearest smoker, 'I'm going to look for Deck Cloud Nine.'

'You do that, love. Let us know if you find the stair.' She winks at her pal and I hear her mutter, 'Aw, bless,' as I close the door to the lounge behind me.

God almighty. I might be the youngest person on the boat but I'm not *five*.

I can see the sign to Deck Cloud Nine, but when I take the carpeted stairway it leads to a locked door on Deck Eight with a polite gold-framed notice about cleaning. *Please use the alternative access via Deck Three.*

That hardly seems worth the effort, so I head for the restaurant on Deck Five instead. On the room plan I'm down for table thirty-two, which is set for two people. But nobody else arrives, so the waiter pulls out the chair for me and flicks a linen napkin onto my lap. He has a very beautiful face and he smiles a lot. It's a slightly condescending smile but he's friendly despite the stiff white jacket and all the gold braid.

There's an empty chair opposite me, and he nods at it sympathetically.

'Would you like company for dinner?' He starts to glance around for another lone diner.

'No!' That sounded a little panic-stricken. 'No,' I say again, as sweetly as I'm able.

'I daresay he'll be joining you later in the cruise,' says the waiter.

I open my mouth to say *I hope not*, but when I turn he's already gone.

It seems I'm not the youngest here, after all. When I first left my cabin I thought I was, owing to the staggering proportion of oldies, but I wasn't looking properly. There's a family two tables away, two boys aged maybe ten and eight with their parents. They seem to know fine they're too young for this lark. They and their mother look as if they're trying desperately to have fun; they're playing cards while they wait for their avocado starter. They steal occasional nervous glances at Father, while he just stares into the middle distance, a half-scowl on his rigid face.

I dislike the father on sight. Viscerally. I try smiling at the older of the two boys, because I think I recognise his face, but he just blinks in a frightened way and goes back to his cards.

I'm in a sulky mood when I leave the dining room. And the weather has worsened, so the ship's tilting a little more. When I'm thrown sideways I have to fling up a hand against the wall to save myself, and suddenly he's there, right in front of me.

His face holds a hint of apology, and he opens his mouth as if to say something. But something bad happened the last time I let him talk, I know it did. Terror pounds in my chest like the memory of a heartbeat, so I turn on my heel and run.

'MARNIE!' He really shouts it this time.

I don't slow down till I'm three decks away and even then I keep walking fast, my eyes on the carpet. It's all sea-shades: turquoise and green and jade, although in a murky carpet-coloured way. It's a lot more cheerful than the actual sea, which if anything has grown duller and greyer since I last looked. Even the blurred smear of mist that passes for a horizon has come closer. Desperate for air, I stick my head out of one of the heavy deck doors, and it nearly blows shut and decapitates me. I have to wrestle against the wind, and when I get out on deck I don't know why I bothered.

I'm outside, I remind myself, *because he's inside.*

The mother with the two boys is out on deck, marshalling them into taking some exercise. They're actually looking a bit happier, now that Father isn't around, and they're playing some kind of shuffleboard game on the rain-soaked timber. I'm almost definitely sure now that I know the boys' faces, though their mother is more forgettable, with her ashy hair and her drawn face. I take a breath to chat to the older boy but Mother takes a sort of step forward and looks so protective, and so defensive, that I change my mind. I wriggle back into a sheltered spot by a lifeboat, and watch the game. I have to pretend to be interested in something.

Then I see the father. He's wearing a heavy anorak, like anybody sensible would be, and he's marching round the corner onto the starboard deck, where we are, and he's looking unsettled. Their heads snap up.

'Come on now, come on.' He tries to herd them, like a jowly sheepdog. 'I didn't know where you were. We've got to stay together.'

There's not much mutinous grumbling from the boys, who gather up their stuff and meekly start to follow him, but Mother gives him a look of such hatred that I sway with shock (the roll of the deck obviously doesn't help). She doesn't say anything, though.

'Well, it's true,' he says, miffed. 'I thought we agreed.'

She shakes her head, not so much as if she's disagreeing; more as if she's disgusted. Maybe they're having marital difficulties. Maybe that's why they're on the boat in the first place: a little family time together. If you ask me, it's not working.

I am so embarrassed to be stuck in the middle of a domestic, but I'm trapped between the lifeboat divot and the rail, and I really don't want to squeeze past them, glaring at each other the way they are. Instead I turn away and stare determinedly at the choppy iron sea, at the wisps of spindrift blown up and flung back in the wind. I'm trying not to hear, because she's shouting at him now, if you can call that low hissing fury a shout. I can't really make out what they're saying, and fortunately they're moving away, sidling down the deck towards the stern like a couple of crabs, arms folded, never taking their beady eyes off each other.

I steal a glance, then look quickly away again because she's raised her voice. Best not to move. Best to stay here, since they've forgotten me, and wait till they've gone altogether.

'You think I don't remember!' she screams. 'But I do!'

'Well—'

'So, do you think I just don't care?'

'No! It's not as if I meant—'

'You think I'm just going to *forgive you*.'

There's a flush of mortification creeping up my neck despite the whipping slash of the wind. Also, there's something else bothering me; it's the way she's talking, like she's turned up the volume of the voices inside my own head.

Suddenly panicked, I clap my hands over my ears. What good that's going to do, I don't know, but I don't want to hear.

Nor do I especially want to be a witness to this quarrel, whatever he's done. The whole ship would be able to hear them by now if it wasn't for the rising scream of the gale. It really is time to slip back inside.

I'm just starting to do that, edging towards the door and putting my hand on its lever, about to wrestle it open, when a violent motion catches the edge of my eye. Something strikes, something stumbles, something falls.

It's nothing more than that, just a shove, or a hard punch maybe. Anyway, when I skip back a step and peer at the squabbling parents, concerned for her, it's not the parents any more. He must have flounced off, it's just Mother.

She's storming up the deck towards me, arms folded tightly across her flimsy wrap dress, hair tossed and tugged by the wind. When she gets to the door she stares at me, as if she's forgotten I was there.

'Hell of a day,' I say brightly, as if I've seen and heard nothing. Poor cow.

She just nods. Her face is flushed and her eyes are burning, but not with tears. With all the strength of rage she yanks the heavy door open.

I follow her in.

Call me fussy, but I don't think 'Bridge Over Troubled Water' is either cheerful or appropriate, especially played badly on that aggravating keyboard by a stocky man with a hairpiece. He's got the full electronic orchestra turned up, with what passes for mandolins, violas, trumpets, drums. I wonder again what on earth I'm doing here when I could be down the municipal park with Bryony and Meg and a Bacardi Breezer carry-out.

Not that I want to wonder too hard.

There's a singer in a cocktail dress leaning on the pretend piano, gazing at the stocky man with adoration. She's all hairspray and sequins and when he finishes with a flourish of chords, she lifts the microphone and launches into 'My Heart Will Go On'.

Even WORSE.

Nobody else seems to mind the theme from *Titanic* and the slightly-too-sharp key, so I rock and roll between tables and blue rinses and make my unsteady way to the bar. I bite my lip and open my mouth to risk asking for something alcoholic, but the barman beats me to it and plonks down a champagne glass. A full one. It has a strawberry in the bottom. Very festive.

He smiles at me. 'No harm in it,' he says.

I pick up the drink and take a mouthful. No, he's not fobbing me off with Appletiser; it zings straight to my head. I fish out the strawberry with a finger and eat it. It is by some way the best strawberry I have ever tasted, but then it is soaked in cava.

'That's nice,' I say.

He doesn't reply, but he's still smiling, and he doesn't charge me.

I say thank you and wander off towards the dining room. Who knew eating could get so boringly relentless? At least I don't seem to be putting on any weight. I suppose that must be down to all the scarpering along corridors and up and down decks when he tries to intercept me.

At least he still hasn't come near the dining room, or not at the same time as me. That would just be beyond awkward.

The ashy mother and her two boys are sitting at the next table to me, and the head waiter is all over them, metaphorically speaking. There's no sign of the father. Mother's cheekbones are flushed again, but this time I think it's with cava and pleasure, not anger. The boys are relaxed, giggling over a Nintendo game. I watch Mother flash a conspiratorial look at the head waiter, who smiles indulgently, and my stomach goes cold.

I watch the doors, expecting the father to walk through them at any moment. But he doesn't. And Mother doesn't seem to be missing him.

I eat a prawn, for something to do, but it's shell-dust in my mouth. I've got a horrible feeling about this. I think about the thump, the shove, the punch, the thing I saw with only a fraction of the edge of my eye. The thing that fell. I think about how nobody would hear a splash in that wind. I think about how her eyes burned. I think, like I didn't think then, about the fact there wasn't a mark on her face.

I don't think he hit her.

I can't eat. She seems so happy. The head waiter is flirting with her, and she's loving it. The ashiness is gone.

I wonder who I can tell. I wonder if anyone will believe me. I think how stupid I'll feel if the father appears at breakfast, having suffered no more than a dodgy stomach.

She leans across to me. Oh, she's all friendly now.

'We've been upgraded!'

'Oh,' I say lamely. 'Oh, that's really nice.'

'Yes it is! We're getting a cabin up on Cloud Nine.' She can hardly contain herself. 'Deck Cloud Nine!'

That's what's so different, then. I'm so obviously

snatching at the wrong end of the boat hook. She's all happy because she's got an upgrade, and a balcony, and a private pool, and a fabulous Observation Lounge. Maybe Father is staying down on Deck Five and that's why she feels so relieved. Perhaps he's sulking, but I'm sure he'll appear at breakfast. Even if the rest of the family don't, even if they're off eating smoked salmon and truffles on Deck Cloud Nine, I'm sure he'll be back here in the regular dining room.

I think about how idiotic I'd feel then, having told the purser what she's done; that she's shoved her husband overboard, and we're sailing on into the fog without him.

I'm back in the photo gallery next morning, nursing a slight cava headache and searching for some sign of the father appearing in the new portraits; Mr Paparazzi was lurking again last night, and there's no escaping him. If the father was around, there'll be photographic evidence.

The thing is, you see, he never did show up at breakfast.

I'm seriously anxious now. There's a nice print of the rest of the family: Mother and boys, laughing into the camera as if they haven't got a care in the world. As if Father hasn't disappeared off a boat in the middle of the ocean.

Or maybe as if he has.

There's been no sign of those three this morning, either, but I expect they're living the high life up on Deck Cloud Nine now.

I'm probably imagining things. He's probably there with them.

But I don't think so.

I decide I should go up and see if I can track him down, just for my peace of mind and for something to do. But when I examine the ship's plan that hangs in reception, then follow what looks like the appropriate stairwell, it takes me up two flights and down one and I'm back in the casino.

I puff out an exasperated sigh. A man in a dinner jacket, gazing gloomily at the roulette wheel, takes no notice. The croupier does; she gives me one of those knowingly sympathetic smiles – all the staff can do them – and spins the wheel again. I hear the *clickety-clickety* of the ball as it slows and jumps, and the man sucks in a hopeful breath.

'No more bets,' says the croupier. 'No more bets.'

I want to confide in her. I want to tell her about the scene on deck and the man who isn't here any more and the family that's lost a member, but as soon as I open my mouth she looks straight at me and winks.

I shut my mouth. I feel very very cold, so although I'm not hungry at all, I turn and head for the dining room and table thirty-two.

It's quiet in there. Funny, but I find that reassuring.

It's like I can feel and hear things around me; not like when I'm surrounded by clicking roulette wheels or twangy keyboard music, by a drawling bingo call or crashing water being flung round the pool. It's like the voices in my head are quiet at last and I can think and remember. More thinking than remembering, to be honest, and it's all to do with what I saw up on deck yesterday. I have the sense that I'm all finished running.

So I don't jump when he sits down opposite me.

I wait till the beautiful waiter has flicked napkins onto our laps, his face smug with delight at our reunion. Even when he's strutted away, though, my new dining companion can't look me in the eye. All he can do is play with his fork.

'I don't know why you thought this was a good idea,' I tell him.

He's lacing and unlacing his fingers now, staring fixedly at them, cracking his knuckles. 'Neither do I. Really. Now that we're here.'

'It's not exactly the weather for it,' I say.

He laughs, but when I don't he shuts up and blushes.

'Your mother's joining us at the next port of call,' he says, as if that's any comfort. As if I'd want her to come too. Insensitive bastard.

'So we're not getting off?'

'No. We pick up the next passengers and turn

round.' At least he's managed to stop talking in capital letters. Like he's calmed down a bit, had time to think. 'It's back-to-back cruises.'

'Lovely.'

'I wanted your mother with us from the start, but, you know.' He swallows. 'There was a delay.'

'You screwed up,' I tell him. 'You couldn't even get this right. Not even this.'

If you knew my dad, you'd know how much he deserved that. He does screw things up. All. The. Time. It's why he gets so unreasonably angry. I never understood that before but I've realised now it's not my fault. It was never my fault.

And as I've made a point of saying: I didn't ask to be here.

'You've been avoiding me,' he says, after a bit.

'Well, that's hardly surprising.'

'I know.' His eyes slide sideways and he nibbles his lip. 'I've been very selfish.'

'But you still want Mum on board too.'

'Yes,' he says. 'Yes, I suppose I'm still being selfish.'

I smirk. That one doesn't even need an answer.

Now that I've sat there and looked him in the eye, it strikes me that it's my turn to be angry. He shouldn't have done what he did. Because it's coming back to me, in lurid snapshot images, what it was he did. There's still a gap in my head where the voices live, a gap between that time he was so angry, angrier than ever, and he found me, and here, now, being on this boat. There's still a void in the middle of the picture, a hole where the pattern's missing – no, not missing, exactly. The pattern's there, the whole picture's there, but I don't know how to look at it, so I'm only looking at the frame and the bits inside the edge. Possibly I don't want to look at the middle yet. I'm avoiding looking.

Besides, it's a big picture. When people say you need to look at 'the big picture', they tend to forget that you can't do that very easily. You can't take it all in at once, not unless you step right back. And if I step right back I'll be in the ocean.

Won't I?

I'd be in the ocean with that other father, the one with the two boys, the One Who Was Pushed. Or was that only in my hyperactive imagination? I frown, remembering, and worrying all over again. I wonder if my own dad's seen him around.

I don't ask, because I need some air very, very badly. I push back my chair and stand up.

'I'm sorry about it all!' he calls after me but, if you ask me, he doesn't sound all that sorry.

The obvious place to go for air is, ironically, the smokers' deck. That's where the friendly women hang out, and I feel the need for some company. The wind is really rising and by now the deckchairs down by the pool are rearranging themselves but, sure enough, the smokers give me welcoming smiles when I shove open the door and stand at the rail, shivering and rubbing my arms.

'Find Deck Cloud Nine, did you?' says one.

I shake my head.

They shake their heads in echo. 'It's a labyrinth, so it is.'

'You need to get used to the ship,' says another. 'You need to get to know it. That's what I heard.'

'You need to accept that you're even on it,' adds another. 'Your trouble is, you don't want to be on this cruise any more than I do.' She extends her pack of Silk Cut. 'Here, have one.'

I shake my head again, embarrassed that I'm so transparent. 'No, thanks.'

'You might as well now,' she says, and laughs a hacking laugh. 'No harm in it.'

That reminds me of the barman who let me have cava, and I'm about to say so when I feel a hand on my elbow. I turn round and it's the eight-year-old, the younger son of the mother who drowned her husband. It occurs to me to say something along these lines until I realise how inappropriate it would be. And I'm not sure.

'I thought you were up on Deck Cloud Nine,' I say.

'I just popped back down,' he says. 'I missed—'

My breath catches. 'Who?'

'I don't... Nobody.' He shrugs, avoiding my eyes. 'I missed it. Just for a bit. I'm OK now. Anyway, I saw you talking to that man.'

'Oh?' I mutter lamely.

'So, you ready yet? Because I can show you the stairs,' he says.

'Oh,' I say, 'OK.'

The woman with the Silk Cut nods encouragingly at me.

'You want to come and see?' I ask her.

'I'm not quite ready.' She smiles with yellow teeth and waves her fag.

'What she means,' her friend says, 'is she's still livid about being on this cruise at all.'

The pair of them burst into that hacking laughter, and one of them chokes, 'Have a nice time!'

The boy climbs the outside staircase just ahead of me, and because it's easier to be blunt with an eight-year-old than with his scary mother, I say, 'I recognise you from somewhere.'

'That'll be the papers.' He nods sagely. 'I'm Nicholas. Nicholas Moore.'

I remember now. I remember those two boys in a digital camera flash, with their mother and father behind them, all grinning on a holiday balcony. I remember that he drugged them and threw them all off that balcony one night, one at a time. *Bump. Bump. Bump.*

And then he jumped after them.

'He isn't my father. He's my stepfather.'

'Oh, right,' I say.

They were such a happy normal family, said one of their neighbours back home.

Speaking of normal families, Dad's waiting at the top of the steps, Deck Seven level, outside a varnished door. He's damp and miserable.

'Are you going upstairs?' he says. 'Please don't. Please don't go without me.'

I hesitate. Nicholas gives him a proper glare, one filled with righteous indignation.

'Marnie,' says Dad, 'can we not talk a bit more? Work this out?'

'Nah,' I say. I look at him, leaning on the rail with his arms defensively folded. 'I already worked it out fine.'

'Anyway, knives,' says the boy, wrinkling his nose. 'It's not like that can be an accident. I mean, you can't even shove three people off a balcony by accident, but honestly. *Knives*.'

I shiver and I touch my throat, feeling the ridge of sawn flesh. I can see the whole picture now; I'm looking at the bit in the middle. It's clear, once I focus properly. The centre of the picture, the heart of the action, is chaotic: scarlet and screaming and terror, and it comes to an end. It's not a nice scene but at least I can look now, make it out. Big picture.

'I'm sorry,' Dad says again. 'I don't know what came over me.'

I doubt that. What came over him must have been unmistakeable, irresistible, like a great grey ocean slumping over his head, washing him away and taking us too.

'You see,' I say, 'the thing is. The thing is, I'm not scared of you any more.'

It's true. I don't feel like that other mother did. There's no need to do anything as dramatic as shove him over the railings. It's just that I'm not scared and I don't need to run.

He can have it out with my mum at the next port of call, when she finally stops breathing and comes on board. I guess they'll have a lot to discuss.

'I don't want to stay down here,' he says plaintively.

I lean forward impulsively and kiss his cheek. It's cold.

'Neither do I, though.'

There are tears in his eyes, but I'm way too inexperienced to tell remorse from self-pity, so I don't try. Anyway, I still haven't forgiven him for the scarlet and the screaming and the terror. And the fact that it all just ends.

The boy Nicholas hauls open the door; he doesn't have to struggle against the wind, since it isn't the least bit stormy up here; it's bright and breezy and the air smells of soap. I follow him inside and there it is, the long flight of stairs: all neatly hoovered carpet, turquoise and jade.

Deck Cloud Nine, says the dinky gold-framed sign.

Of course it is. Obvious when you know what you're looking for.

Obvious when you stop running.

THE RECEIVING END

Malorie Blackman

THE RECEIVING END

Where should I start?

I have a sister. I guess that's as good a place as any to start. I have a sister. And I think...I think I killed her.

Am I going to hell? Is that why I'm here, to plead my case?

I know...I know I deserve nothing else but before I'm sent there, can I tell my side of the story? Please?

Please?

My name is Victoria. Everyone calls me Vicky – except for my dad. He used to call me Tori. My sister's name is Antonia. All her friends call her Toni. That's why I prefer Vicky, otherwise it gets too confusing. When we were born, Mum wanted our names to be completely different, but Dad wanted our names to be almost the same. So Victoria and

Antonia was a compromise they could both live with. Dad could call us Tori and Toni. He likes mind puzzles and crosswords and whimsical things like that. My sister and I looked as alike as two grains of sand on a beach. We weren't just identical twins but super-identical.

No one stood a chance, really.

'You two were probably swapped around at least a dozen times before you could walk!' Dad used to tell us that all the time.

When we were babies, not even Mum and Dad could tell us apart. For all I know, I could've been the one who was christened Antonia. Maybe me and my sister got swapped around and Antonia led the life I should've had and I got stuck with her life, all because no one could tell the difference between us.

When we started school, Mum wanted one of us to have short hair and the other to keep it long to make it easier for the teachers – and probably Mum and Dad as well – to tell us apart. I liked my hair long. Antonia didn't care one way or the other, until she knew I did. Then she had one of her tantrums, screaming that she didn't want to have her hair cut – ever. She wouldn't let up until Mum and Dad gave in. My hair was cropped short into a pixie cut, which didn't suit my face, and I wasn't allowed to grow it out until I was twelve going on thirteen, by which time I think my hair had given up trying to grow cos it'd been cut so often. After that, I could never get it to grow past my shoulders.

I was very different to Antonia. Everyone said so. She was a bitch and then some if she didn't get her own way. A lot of people at school were afraid of her. She'd walk down the corridor with her mates and everyone else would get out of their way. People would part like the Red Sea. Not out of respect or awe or anything. Out of fear. And Antonia loved it, she revelled in it. The funny thing is, even though we're twins, no one ever got out of my way when I walked down the corridor. I guess everyone at school could tell us apart by the friends around us. And a lot of the time, I walked alone. Oh, I had mates, don't get me wrong. But I didn't need to make a constant show of how popular I was the way my sister did.

I can't remember a time when it was any different. I was the quiet one – Victoria the mouse, Victoria the shadow. I just kept my head down and got on with my work, or stuck my head in a book. Antonia was the life and soul, if you know what I mean. She never cracked open a book. I'm sure she was allergic to them. I can't remember the last time I saw her reading for pleasure. My school grades were always better than hers. Isn't it funny how two people can look so alike and yet be so completely different?

To be honest, in secondary school Antonia and I kept out of each other's way. We didn't have much in common. And even less when Dad left us, because Antonia had always been his favourite and then he was gone. Once Dad left, as far as Antonia was concerned, the brakes were off. I know a lot of what she did was because she was hurting, but her way of dealing with it was to take it out on the person closest to her – and that was me. I know… I know we weren't great friends or anything, but we were… are sisters. That counts for something, at least it does to me.

But I never realised until too late just how much she hated me.

I'm not making excuses. I know I'm partly responsible for what happened to her. But let me just say this, it was an accident.

I never meant to hurt Antonia. She's my sister. I would never harm her deliberately. You do know that, don't you? I never meant for anyone to get hurt.

But here I am.

And I'm scared…

I admit it. I'm terrified.

Is it true what they say about hell? That it's fire and sulphur and torture and suffering. I don't know why, but that's not my idea of hell, not a twenty-first century hell. If you don't mind me saying, that sounds a little… old-fashioned. But maybe that's the point? But if that is what hell is like then God knows I don't want to go there.

So what happens now?

I guess I'll have to accept whatever fate is waiting for me. But first, if... When you see my sister, could you tell her that I... Never mind. It doesn't matter anymore. I guess none of that old stuff matters anymore.

Or does it?

When I was ten, nearly eleven, I lay on the hardwood floor of our living room, colouring in a picture of a lion I'd just drawn. I was proud of that lion, it was the best one I'd ever done. Dad was so impressed he said that if I coloured it in very carefully, he would stick it to our fridge door. So I was determined to make it the very best lion I could. I lay on my stomach, my coloured pencils fanned out on the wooden floor around my picture and I moved my light-brown pencil very carefully across the paper, making sure never to go over my lion's outline, making sure not to leave any gaps. The early afternoon's summer sunshine filled almost every corner of the room and stroked the back of my head like warm hands. It was a lovely feeling. And Dad liked my drawing. I lay on the floor, smiling to myself because it was sunny outside and I felt sunny inside. I was so engrossed in my picture that I had no inkling of what was about to happen next.

My sister, Antonia, jumped off the sofa and landed with both feet on my outstretched arm. A crack, a snap, a moment's stunned silence – and then I *screamed*. Dad came running into the room, crying, 'What's the matter? What's happened?'

But I couldn't speak for the roaring pain devouring my body.

And as for my arm . . .

My forearm was no longer straight but a funny V shape. Blood was pooling on the wood beneath my arm and a jagged piece of bone was sticking through my skin. Just the sight of it made me howl even louder. I looked up at Dad, and the horror-stricken expression on his face made me scream harder.

Antonia kneeled in front of me, wailing, 'It was an accident! It was an accident!'

After Dad had phoned for an ambulance, he spent more time with Antonia trying to calm her down than he did with me.

My arm was so badly broken I had to wear a cast for well over two months. But the up side was I got lots of attention. Antonia didn't like that. But I guess she had the last laugh, because my right arm was never the same afterwards. I had all kinds of physiotherapy and did every exercise I was given, but my arm was never as strong as it'd been before. There was a weakness in it, not all the time but often enough to never let me forget what my sister had done.

I guess I became a bit over-protective of my arm. When playing rounders or football, I instinctively turned the left side of my body forward to protect my right arm, or I'd twist and place my right forearm behind my back. Of course, Antonia noticed what I was doing before I did. She started challenging me to arm-wrestling contests and giving my right arm wrist twists. Never my left arm, just my right. And, of course, she was careful to make sure she only tormented me when Mum and Dad weren't looking – but I was used to that.

One good thing came out of my broken arm – Mrs Farringdon, my next-door neighbour.

Before the 'accident', Antonia and I sometimes saw her watching us from her bedroom window as we walked to and from school.

'Nosy old cow.' What started off as my sister's muttered comments to me, soon became verbal abuse silently mouthed up at our neighbour every time we passed her house. I begged Antonia not to, but she never listened to me. I guess she hated the thought that anyone was watching her. I must admit, it kind of got on my nerves that Mrs Farringdon had nothing better to do than to spy on me and my sister. I mean, what did she think we were going to do? Steal the lavender out of her front garden?

But when I broke my arm and I needed to take a few days off school, Mum and Dad couldn't afford to take the time away from work to stay with me. So they asked Mrs Farringdon if she could baby-sit. And, to the surprise of us all, she said yes.

'You are to be on your very best behaviour for Mrs Farringdon, d'you hear?' Mum warned me for the umpteenth time before taking me round to our neighbour's house.

The last thing I wanted was to be looked after by the pensioner next door. That was nothing short of my idea of hell.

'Serves you right!' laughed my sister when she heard. 'You two suit each other. Enjoy!'

I dragged my feet as Mum took me round to Mrs Farringdon's. The moment the old woman opened the door Mum launched in, 'I can't thank you enough for agreeing to do this, Freydis. It's so kind of you. And I've told Vicky to behave herself.'

'No problem, Zandra. I'm only glad I can help,' said Mrs Farringdon, though her gaze never left me.

It was so strange seeing her up close like this when I'd only ever seen her watching us through one of her windows before. She had piercing brown eyes which burned straight through me, making me feel like I'd done something wrong when I hadn't. Mum kissed me on the cheek and left me with Mrs Farringdon. I watched Mum head to the car to drive Antonia to school. My sister grinned at me, loving the situation I was in. Alone with an OAP. This day was going to last *forever*.

Mrs Farringdon very gently but firmly closed her front door.

'So, Vicky, what would you like to do first?' my neighbour asked. 'You can help me in the garden or you can help me paint the spare bedroom.'

'I can't do either. I've got a broken arm,' I pointed at it, just in case she was having trouble seeing the plaster cast and the sling.

'Nonsense. A broken arm won't stop you from doing anything you want to do, unless you let it,' said Mrs Farringdon.

It sounded to me like she just wanted some cheap labour and someone with only one hand was better than no one at all.

How much was this day going to suck?

'I'll help in the garden, please,' I decided reluctantly. The garden sounded like the lesser of two evils.

'Fine,' she smiled. 'And do please call me Freydis.'

Freydis... So I had heard Mum correctly. I considered her name, rolling the syllables around on my tongue. Freydis. 'I've never heard that name before. I like it.'

'Thank you,' Mrs Farringdon smiled. 'I was named after Freydis, the brave but brutal warrior daughter of Erik the Red. She was very handy with an axe and a sword. It's quite a name to live up to. But in my youth, I've been told I was quite formidable.'

She still was! I looked up at her. 'Your name suits you,' I decided.

'I know,' she smiled, her eyes twinkling.

Freydis led the way through her kitchen and out into her immaculate garden with its precision flowery borders and lawn that looked like it had been cut with scissors rather than a lawn mower.

'Kneel down over there on that garden mat and pull out anything that doesn't have a flower at the top of it,' she directed.

So that's what I did, whilst Freydis chatted away. And after a couple of minutes, she had me smiling. And after five minutes I was laughing out loud. And by the time we sat down to have sandwiches for our lunch, Freydis and I were friends.

It was as simple and as straightforward as that.

'Freydis, d'you mind if I ask you something?' I began tentatively. I didn't want to upset her but I needed to know.

'Ask away, dear.'

'Why d'you watch me and my sister when we go to school?'

Freydis's smile faded. 'I'm looking out for you.'

I frowned. 'Looking out for me and Antonia? Why?'

'No, not your sister. You,' said Freydis.

'*Me?* I don't understand.'

There was a long pause. At first I wondered if I'd said something wrong – though for the life of me I couldn't figure out what.

'I was a twin too,' Freydis said at last. 'My sister and I never saw eye to eye, either.'

'Antonia and I get on just fine,' I denied, embarrassed heat rising up my neck to my cheeks.

Freydis raised an eyebrow.

'Sometimes,' I amended with a mumble.

Freydis considered me carefully. 'D'you want to know what I think? Your sister is jealous of you.'

I stared at her, my eyes as wide as hubcaps. Antonia was jealous of me? In which parallel universe?

'You don't believe me, but I'm right,' said Freydis.

'What on earth makes you think that?'

Freydis's jaw moved like she was chewing on the words before she could spit them out.

'I've seen the way she looks at you,' she said at last. 'I recognise the way she treats you.'

Freydis looked away, casting her glance anywhere but at me.

'Why didn't you and your sister get on?' I asked.

Freydis inhaled slowly before turning back to me, her dark-green eyes clouded with sadness. 'My sister Freya and I were close when we were young. As we grew older we drifted apart.'

'Why?' I couldn't help asking. Freydis was the only other twin I'd ever met. I don't know what I was hoping for, maybe some clue as to why Antonia and I descended from sisters to somewhere well below friends. In all the books I'd ever read twins were always so close, like they shared a mystical bond or something. But as far as I could see, that was only in stories.

Freydis sighed. 'Freya was the quiet one, the clever one. I wasn't. She didn't mind, but I did. It seemed like everyone wanted me to be more like her, no one ever suggested that Freya became more like me. So we grew up and grew older and grew to have less and less in common, except the fact that we were twins. And I see the same thing happening between you and your sister.'

'Oh, I see.'

And I did see, but more than Freydis. Antonia and I weren't just growing apart. There was more to it. But I wasn't prepared to analyse it any deeper than that.

Freydis placed a gentle hand on my shoulder.

'I want you to promise me something,' she said after a long pause.

'What?'

'That you'll live your own life, not your sister's. If there's something you really want and she doesn't or vice versa, promise me that you'll follow your heart and not your sister.'

'I promise,' I shrugged. To be honest, I didn't really have a clue what Freydis was talking about, but I figured it wouldn't do any harm to promise anyway.

When my arm got better, I still made a point of popping in to see Freydis most afternoons on my way home from school. And she was always glad to see me. She asked me the same questions as Mum and Dad, about my day, my friends, my school, about my hopes and dreams for the future. And every day she asked the one thing that no one else ever did. She asked how my sister was treating me. And I always told her the truth, shared with her the things that I couldn't share with anyone else – the public put-downs, the name calling, the contents of my bag being dumped into the toilet. The list went on.

And, as if Antonia's behaviour was somehow my fault, I went out of my way to be kind to all the other people my sister ridiculed or bullied. I wasn't trying to be a goody-goody or suck up to anyone, I guess I was just trying to be a balance for my sister, which of course just made things worse between the two of us.

But none of that mattered when I won a full scholarship to attend Silverdene Girls' School. Freydis was the only one who knew just how happy I was when I got my acceptance letter. I was going to be at a different school to my sister. Here was my chance to move out from beneath the weight and darkness of my sister's shadow. Now, at last, I could be my own person instead of merely Antonia's twin sister. But Antonia persuaded Mum and Dad that we should go to the same school, that it wouldn't be fair to either of us if we were split up. I tried to tell them that I wanted nothing else, but parents see what they want to see and hear what they want to hear. At least, mine did. They heard Antonia. They didn't hear me.

I went to the same school as Antonia.

And, not long after, Dad left. He met someone else and left a note saying he had fallen out of love with Mum and couldn't cope with the atmosphere in our home. He was luckier than the rest of us. He could pack up all the good bits of his life and head out the door, leaving what was left behind. And when Dad went, my sister's bullying got worse – only now she didn't bother to disguise it. If Antonia tried it on at home, Mum would separate us, yelling, 'Why can't the two of you get on? Don't you think I'm unhappy enough without both of you adding to it?'

School was a different story, but I learned to deal with it. What choice did I have? I dreaded school and I hated my house. Freydis's home became my oasis.

There was one strange incident that sticks in my mind, though. It happened about a year before the accident. Juliet, one of Antonia's newer minions, tried to follow my sister's example by picking on me. She shoved me so hard against a wall that I was winded and knew I'd have bruises up and down my back for at least a week. She was only doing it as a way to get in with my sister, but Antonia did something none of us expected. She freaked. Antonia grabbed Juliet by her hair and slammed her against a cubicle door in the girls' toilets.

'Don't you ever, as long as you live, touch my sister again.' Antonia wasn't just annoyed, she was wild-eyed furious. Flecks of spit foamed at the corners of her mouth as she glared at Juliet.

'But, Toni, you do it,' Juliet protested, rubbing the back of her head where her hair had been yanked.

'Vicky is *my* sister. I'm not going to let you or anyone else touch her,' Antonia declared with some kind of perverse logic that escaped me. She and Juliet started arguing about it. I used the opportunity to grab my bag and run.

Freydis was the only one who heard that story too.

So that was it, my so-called life, because I could never get away from my sister.

Until something inside me finally snapped.

It was the fifth year anniversary of the day Dad walked out. Antonia and I were both at the same bus stop but I stood as far away from her as was possible without being in danger of missing the bus should it eventually decide to pull up. Even though I wasn't looking at her, I knew Antonia was watching me. My nape began to prickle and beads of sweat, sharp as briars, stung my forehead. My sister was about to start something, I could feel it. I could always feel it. I could've been on the other side of the planet and I would've known that my sister was thinking of me – and not in a good way. Antonia started to head in my direction. I knew that without having to look. Hoisting my full-to-overflowing school bag further up onto my shoulder, I turned and headed away from Antonia. I didn't run, I couldn't run because of my heavy bag, but I didn't want to get into anything. Not today. I was feeling bad enough already.

'Where're you going?' asked Antonia, easily catching up with me.

'I'm going to buy myself a drink,' I told her, risking a glance in her direction.

My fears were confirmed. Eyes narrowed, lips pursed, Antonia was obviously hurting and she wanted to share. I looked about, seeking some means of escape. The bus to take me to school had just turned the corner but was still a hundred metres down the road. I tried to carry on walking, but my sister grabbed my arm and pulled me round.

'Antonia, don't . . .' I didn't have a chance to say much more than that.

'You ruin everything,' Antonia told me softly. 'Dad left because of you.'

'That's a lie.'

'No, he told me before he left that he couldn't live with you and Mum any more. He said that once you passed the entrance exam to get into Silverdene all you did was look down your nose at him, at all of us. He said that you'd turned into a right snob.'

'You're a liar, Toni. Dad would never have said anything like that about me.'

'What makes you so sure?' my sister asked scornfully.

'Because if he had, it wouldn't have taken you five years to cast it up to me,' I replied, just as angry as Toni now. 'You want to know the real reason Dad left? Because he couldn't wait to get away from you. You know why I was so desperate to go to Silverdene? Because *I* couldn't wait to be away from you, either. Your so-called friends only hang around you because they're too scared to turn their backs. If you were to die tomorrow, the only emotion you'd elicit from anyone who knows you would be a huge sigh of relief...'

With a cry almost like a wounded animal, Antonia leaped at me. But I was ready for her. I turned my body to the side and pushed her away from me. Antonia tried to twist round but her forward momentum kept her falling. Her feet were half on the pavement, half in the gutter of the road. Her arms spun like mini windmills. Flailing wildly, she managed to grab hold of the strap of my school bag, pulling me forward.

And the bus was almost on top of us...

For a fraction of a second I considered slipping my bag off my shoulder and letting my sister fall. D'you understand? That thought actually went through my head. That's why I can't forgive myself. The bus's horn was blaring out incessantly. Somewhere in the background, above the sound of my heart thundering, I heard the scream of the bus's brakes. The bus was little more than a metre away now. I snatched at Antonia to pull her back. I swear I was trying to pull her out of the way of the bus but in her panic she grabbed me and pulled me forward. And we both fell.

That's the last thing I remember.

Did Antonia die as well?

I don't know. I'm not so sure, but I think so.

So here I am.

Is this the first or the fifth or the fifty-millionth time I've had to relive my life up to and including the accident? I can't remember, but I don't think this is the first time I've had to relive my memories.

But the strange thing is, I don't mind. At first I thought I would, but I don't. For a start, I never feel that final fall. Or what must've come afterwards. I've never felt it, not once. I relive my life and concentrate on the good things, the positive things. Like all the times I popped round to see Freydis and how happy she was to see me. And, the peculiar thing is, I *feel* her happiness. It rises up inside and fills me to overflowing and it makes me feel sort of . . . calm inside. Content. I think of the hugs I gave Mum when Dad left and I live through those moments feeling the little bit of comfort Mum felt when I held her. I think of all the jokes I made in my various classes to make my friends and my teachers laugh and it's like being on the receiving end. At first I was too scared, but now I sometimes even think about my sister – like when she jumped on my arm and said it was an accident.

It wasn't.

We both knew that.

But I think of that moment, I breathe in every second of it and wait to relive the excruciating agony I felt, but it never arrives. So where did all that pain go? Not just the physical pain of having my arm broken, but the pain of always knowing right from the start that my sister had done it on purpose.

The receiving end . . .

It took me a while to understand.

All the miseries I'd inflicted and all the joys I'd given to others when I was alive were now all being passed back to me like a baton to experience as my own. I guess that's why I never feel the pain of my arm being broken, or the final agony of falling into the path of the oncoming bus. I closed my eyes after my death, waiting to be exiled to a burning hell and hoping to be delivered to a cool heaven. It took me forever to realise that those places didn't exist, that we each make our own heaven and our own hell through the things we do and the things we say to others – and then we have to live and die and live again for all eternity with every one of our actions. I don't know for certain whether or not Antonia survived our fall. But even if I'm wrong and she did, her time will come. That's life's only guarantee.

And, as for me, I get to be with Mum and Freydis and my friends any time I want. I can even be with my dad when I want. I get to relive special moments with each of them.

I am on the receiving end and I am content.

THE FALLEN

Sally Nicholls

THE FALLEN

Pretty much everyone I love is going straight to burning hell, so sometimes I wonder why I'm trying so hard to get into heaven.

'The devil has all the best musicians,' my dad used to say, but there are times when I think he has all the best people too. My friend Leah, Mr Baksh from the corner shop who used to give me free lollipops when I was little, even the beautiful Jack Harper in Year Ten, who Leah and I are planning on marrying when we've worked out a way to get him to notice us. I used to think I could convert all these people to Catholicism like my mum did my dad, and that then they'd be safe, but so far I haven't even managed to convert Leah. I took her to mass once when we were about eleven, and she spent the whole time trying to make Michael Connor blush and giggling at Father James's moustache.

I should probably never have taken Leah to mass. If you're told about Catholicism and you *still* don't believe in God, you suffer far worse torments after you're dead. Leah just laughs at me when I try and explain to her.

'You don't really believe all that fairy-tale crap, do you?' she says.

'You believe in ghosts,' I say. 'And horoscopes.'

She laughs again.

'Oh, ghosts are real enough. And since ghosts are real, the Bible can't be, right?'

I wish I believed in ghosts. All last year I tried to believe, and I used to listen for one at night when I couldn't sleep, but I never saw so much as a shadow or heard so much as a footstep in the hall.

Leah thinks hell is a big joke.

'Come on,' she said last week, waving a cigarette in front of my nose. 'Jesus didn't have a problem with cigarettes, did he? The Pope hasn't tacked on an eleventh commandment? *Lizzie shalt not have fun with Leah, or do anything except say prayers ever, ever again?*'

'Ha ha,' I said, and I took the cigarette off her. Cigarettes aren't a sin, but they are horrible. Leah's cigarette made me want to throw up. I kind of liked the horribleness, though. It was a bit like punching something when you're angry – it hurts, but it stops you feeling like you're about to explode inside.

Smoking Leah's cigarette made me feel sick and slightly wicked, but even that was better than feeling like Lizzie.

'I wish I could stop being me,' Dad used to say sometimes, and I never understood what he meant. How could you be anyone except yourself?

I get it now.

Leah doesn't know what hell means, that's why she thinks it's funny. If I could explain it to her properly, she wouldn't laugh. We had a visiting priest last month who spent the whole sermon talking about hell.

'Why would a loving God send His children to hell?' he said. 'Why would a God who loves His children abandon them? But God doesn't want to send us to hell, we make that choice for ourselves. God gave us the greatest of all gifts – the will to choose whether to follow him or to go our own way. And *because* we have free will, we can choose to turn away from Him. We can ignore His commandments and we can suffer the consequences.'

I started humming very high and loud inside my head, but I could still hear the priest. I wrapped my arms around my stomach and leaned forward so that my forehead was resting on the pew in front of us. I concentrated very hard on the pew-back, counting the water-spots and cracks in the wood. Mum was staring at the back of Maureen Allen's hat. Her face had that dead look on it again.

'What is heaven?' the priest was saying in his voice like a church bell. 'Heaven is communion with God, with the greatest love that any of us can imagine. Heaven is the consummation of our years of longing and loneliness. It is the very reason for which we were created. And hell is that love and that bliss snatched away for ever. All our lives Jesus is there when we want Him. Jesus is there when we need Him. But if we do not cleave to him on earth, Jesus does not ask us to live with Him in heaven. In hell, He leaves sinners alone for the first time in their lives. In hell, sinners call out in an agony of loneliness, "Save me, Father, save me! Whatever you want, I'll do it." But Jesus says, "Depart from me, you cursed, into the eternal fire!" From that fire no man can escape. He will spend eternity in an agony of longing and loneliness, which will never be appeased.'

Leah doesn't understand what it means, knowing God is with you. But I do, and so did my dad. As I listened, I had this picture in my head, very small and very clear. A picture of my dad in a prison cell, with no door and no window, utterly alone, forever and ever. My dad, beating on the walls, calling, 'I'm sorry, God. Forgive me!' And God at the other side of a chasm as wide as the universe, not even hearing his voice.

Mum stood up suddenly. She pushed past the people in our pew, her fingers clenched pink and white around her white leather handbag. A few heads turned as she *clip-clip-clipped* out down the side of the church, the sound of her high-heeled Sunday shoes echoing up to the roof. I squeezed past an old man with angry eyes and ran out after her.

'Imagine—' the priest was saying, and I imagined a black devil striking him with Satanic lightning and killing him dead on the spot.

Outside the church, Mum was leaning against the wall. Her hands were shaking as she tried to light a cigarette, and tears were spurting out of her eyes. Her face was red. She was making little gasping noises as if she was choking.

'He didn't know, Mum,' I said. 'He wouldn't know.'

'God!' said Mum. She shook the cigarette lighter in a sudden fury. 'God, Lizzie.'

'Here.' I took the cigarette lighter from Mum, trying not to care that she'd taken God's name in vain. I can only worry about so many people at once. The lighter wouldn't spark, and I felt the tears pooling in my eyes as I struggled with it. At last it caught, and Mum held her cigarette out to the flame. Her hand was shaking so much that it took three goes before the cigarette lit. She took a long, slow drag, her chest still shuddering.

'It wasn't true, Mum, was it?' I asked. 'What he said – about Jesus – that wasn't true? If someone lived a good life, like Dad did—?' I stopped. Mum looked down at the scrubby grass, all messed up with cigarette ends and sweet papers.

'Lizzie,' she said. 'Promise me you'll always be a good girl. You'll go to mass and pray to God and do what the priest says – you promise me. If anything happened to you and I even *thought*—'

'I promise,' I said. I could feel the tears rising behind my eyes again, and I blinked them back.

'Thank God,' said Mum. She drew in another long, slow, smoky breath.

'Enough,' she said, half to herself. 'Enough.'

Mum still has the curtain rail up in her bedroom. It's an iron one, with curly bits on the end, and dark, red curtains. I wanted her to change it, but I didn't know how to ask. I'd change the curtains too, if I was her.

After Dad died, Mum started sleeping in the spare room. Their bedroom has this empty feel about it now. Dad's dressing gown still hangs from the peg behind the door, and the book he was reading when he died sits on top of the bookcase with a bookmark halfway through, next to a packet of razor blades and a stack of letters saying things like his library books are overdue and he needs to make an appointment with the opticians.

The room is like a set from a film that ran out of money before the story was finished. What's happened to the man in the photograph? Where's he gone? Where's the woman whose earrings sit in a sad little heap on the bedside cabinet? Who's the girl trapped in the mirror? Will she ever get out?

My dad killed himself here. He waited until I was away on a Geography trip and Mum was at work, then he hanged himself from the curtain rail. A neighbour saw his shadow in the window and called an ambulance. So I never had to see him hanging, and Mum didn't, either. And I know I ought to feel grateful, but actually what I feel is cheated. I watched my dad go through so much. I used to sit and roll him cigarettes while he chain-smoked, and watch old films with him late at night when he couldn't sleep, and now it's like I came nearly all the way with him and then missed the end of the story. I've got a picture in my head, clear as glass, of how he must have looked – like a man I saw in a film once, body turning slowly against the glass, head lolling, toes turned down. I saw his body at the funeral parlour, but it wasn't the same. He was wearing his wedding and funeral suit, and he didn't look like my dad at all.

Nobody knows what happens to suicides after they die. The question is choice. Did Dad know what choice he was making? Because if he didn't – if he was ill, or mad, or just so messed up in his head that he didn't understand what he was doing any more, then it's not his fault. Nor would it be his fault if his choice had been taken away from him. Soldiers bleeding to death in the Somme, unborn babies who'll kill themselves and their mothers if they're born, sick people whose brains are so muddied with pain that they've lost the memory of what it feels like to think long and cool and clear. Nobody likes it when those people kill themselves, or others kill them. But God understands. God forgives.

The other question is desire. Did Dad want to die? Did he think we'd be happier without him? That we'd spend the life-insurance money on a holiday to Bermuda? (We didn't.) See, he used to talk like that sometimes, and if he killed himself because he thought his death would make us happy, then that death was a sin.

Some people reckon if you sin badly enough you go straight to hell – do not pass God, do not collect two hundred pounds. Other people, like Ms Hathaway at school, think everyone gets a chance to go to purgatory. Even if you're an arms dealer or a torturer or someone.

'Because arms dealers and torturers are people too,' she says. 'God doesn't abandon people without offering them a leg up.'

Ms Hathaway would say Dad is in purgatory, or at least that he was offered the chance to go there. And then once he'd atoned for his sins, he could get into heaven.

Which is all very well, but I'd like to know for sure. There's only so much 'nobody knows' I can take when it comes to people I love.

Ms Hathaway is my favourite teacher. She teaches maths and religious studies, which Leah says is a dossy subject, but I like it because in school RS everything is so clear. *What do Jews think about pork? They're against. What do Muslims think about pork? They're against too. What do Humanists think about pork? They couldn't care less.* It's safe and easy, with no smoky places around the edges through which fathers and best friends and broken angels might or might not fall through the cracks.

Today, we're doing euthanasia.

'My mum keeps trying to give me that, miss!' says Jack, but no one laughs.

Ms Hathaway says we're going to do a debate.

'Because it's a complex issue.'

The way we're supposed to resolve this complex issue is by putting Jack and Leah on one table as the 'against' panel and Amy and Ellie on the other as the 'for'. Then we're supposed to ask them questions and argue with them.

Like most things in our school, though, it doesn't work. *Nobody* thinks euthanasia is a bad idea. Not even the 'against' panel.

'It's *stupid*, miss,' Leah says. She flops forward

across the table and flaps her hand about, to show just how stupid it is. She's wearing a peaked hat in purple corduroy and so much silver eye shadow that she looks like she's lost a boxing match to a pixie. 'Why shouldn't you kill yourself if you want to? If you're going to die anyway, what difference does it make?'

'Well, several major world religions say it makes a difference,' says Ms Hathaway. 'So, why? Think about it.'

'Because they're stupid, miss,' says Leah. 'Because they believe what some stupid book tells them instead of using their brains.'

It's last lesson on Friday, which is why we're doing a debate instead of proper work, but it's hard getting people to take RS seriously any time. You'd think Leah would have more tact, given as how her best friend is a Catholic, and we all know Ms Hathaway is too. But Ms Hathaway wouldn't still be here if she took offence at what kids said about God.

'*Somebody* must have an idea,' she says, and she looks straight at me. 'Lizzie?'

That's right, pick on me. Just because I'm religious.

'Because life is sacred,' I say, in as small a voice as it's possible to get away with when being interrogated by a teacher. I look down at my desk, digging at a hole with my biro. I half expect Ms Hathaway to tell me off – she's quite strict about things like graffiti –

but she just looks relieved that someone is disagreeing with Leah.

'And?'

I shrug.

'I dunno.'

I do know, but I don't want to say. I duck my head lower, letting my hair fall forward over my face. I look ridiculous. I feel the tears well up behind my eyes, and I suck my lips in, biting on them hard from the inside to stop myself crying. I never used to cry all the time like this. Surely Ms Hathaway can see I don't want to answer?

'Why is life sacred?' says Ms Hathaway. I don't say anything. 'Lizzie?'

'Because!' I've never shouted at a teacher before, especially not a nice one like Ms Hathaway. 'Because you can't go around killing people, even yourself. You can't. It's . . . It's like killing God.' A few kids giggle, but I ignore them. 'And it's against God's law, and you'll be sent to hell, and—' And suddenly I'm crying, right in the middle of RS, with the whole class watching with their mouths open.

Ms Hathaway gawps at me too, which is frankly rude in a teacher, then she looks over at Mr Hopkins, who is Connor's support worker. Mr Hopkins gets up and says, 'Right, you lot. Murdering the infirm, any more problems we can think of?' And Ms Hathaway is leading me out of the room, with Leah running after us, lugging our school bags, coats and RS handouts – obviously hoping that crying-in-the-hall might run until the end of school.

Ms Hathaway sits me on a bench, and sends Leah off for some loo paper. Leah brings back an entire roll, which is going to leave someone in trouble. She hands it to Ms Hathaway and says, 'Her dad killed himself, miss. And she thinks we're all going to burn in hell. Except you and her, probably.' Which at least is direct, although doesn't say much for the confidences of best friends forever, or whatever we're supposed to be.

Ms Hathaway makes a sort of *a-mmm* noise, and passes me some bunched-up loo roll. She and Leah wait until I've stopped crying, then Ms Hathaway says, 'Suicides don't necessarily end up in hell, Lizzie.'

'I *know*!' I say. It's bad enough dealing with theological problems battering about in my head all day, without having to put up with them in lessons too.

'Hell's for people who reject God. I *know*. And my dad didn't reject God. He loved God. He just—' The tears start falling again. 'He just wasn't strong enough. I know. And . . .' And the rest of the sentence hangs there unsaid, the worst thought of all, the one I don't dare tell even Leah, *What if I'm not strong enough, either?* What if I try all my life to serve God, and then whatever it was that overtook my dad overtakes me as well and it all comes to nothing?

Ms Hathaway looks at me and Leah for a while. Then she says, 'The Greek word for sin . . .'

Leah starts fishing in her jacket pocket, which is where she keeps a bottle of nail varnish especially for teacher monologues.

'Well, actually there are several words meaning sin in the Bible.' Ms Hathaway carries on as though she hasn't noticed. '*Anamartetos*, *proamartano* . . . and *hamartia*. Do you know what *hamartia* means?'

Ms Hathaway always does this. Acts like everyone she meets has degrees in maths and theology, like she does.

'It means to miss the mark,' she says. 'As in archery – to aim at a target and fall short. Or to make a mistake on a maths problem— Are-you-still-listening-to-me-Leah-Tallis?'

'Oh, yeah. Sorry.' Leah starts and pushes up the brim of her hat, to show how much she's still listening. Her dark eyes appear again under her spiky black hair. 'You're saying it's sinful ever to do anything difficult, like maths, and we should all just stick to one plus one equals two forever, right?'

'Don't be sharp, Leah,' says Ms Hathaway. 'You might cut yourself. Though sadly there are some Christians who would agree with you. No. It means that if you need to learn something – about God, about yourself – sometimes God pushes the target further back, further than you ever thought you could shoot. And in learning how to hit that target, sometimes you lose an arrow or two. But better to lose an arrow than, as Leah here says, to spend your whole life shooting right in front of your nose.'

'My dad didn't just lose an arrow,' I say, sadly. 'He shot himself in the neck.'

'He must have been shooting in a hell of a fog,' says Leah. She's got her feet up on the bench opposite and she's painting her nails in the regulation school colours, lime green and baby pink.

I know that everyone thinks their dad is brilliant, but mine really was. He was what my mum used to call a broken saint. She meant that there were lots of things wrong with him: he drank too much after he'd told my mum he'd drive, so we couldn't get home; he used to work and work at something and then just give up right before he was finished; he'd spend money we didn't have on things we didn't need, like holidays to Ireland, or the doll's house I wanted and wanted when I was seven, or the red dress that made my mum look like a film star, but cost more than my entire wardrobe put together.

There were a lot of things wrong with my dad, but there were also moments of such grace that they took your breath away. There was the time he drove me round every supermarket and newsagent in town in his van – all these poky little corner shops in the middle of nowhere – so I could fill a glass jar with two thousand, one hundred and eighty-three Smarties for the guess-how-many-Smarties-there-are-in-a-jar stall at the church fête. Or the time he took a homeless woman into Henri's – the best restaurant in town – and told her to order whatever she fancied.

'Why didn't you just buy her a sandwich like everyone else?' my mum wailed when he told her about it. My dad was a painter and decorator, so it wasn't like *we* had the money to eat in Henri's.

'Because,' he said, with his guilty-dog grin. 'Everyone needs a red-letter day now and then.'

It wasn't just me who thought my dad was wonderful, either. After the funeral Mum got about two hundred letters from people saying how amazing he was. He'd get piles of Christmas cards from people we'd never heard of. Mum would go, 'Eileen? Who's Eileen, darling? And why is she thanking you for a wonderful evening in May?' And Dad would go, 'Eileen! You know Eileen. Bred tortoises. Funny nose. She's a friend of Gary's step-aunt, remember?' And it would turn out he was talking about this eighty-four-year-old woman we'd met at a party and I'd thought was dreadfully dull, but who'd actually been parachuted into occupied Holland during the Second World War and still had the shell casings to prove it.

He wasn't perfect, my dad. But I bet Jesus's family didn't like him much sometimes, either, running off to preach in the street and abandoning the family carpentry business. I bet St Francis's wife thought he was an idiot, buying all the caged birds in the shop and setting them free. It doesn't mean they weren't wonderful, just because they were idiots sometimes too.

When I get home from school today, Mum has the gas fire on and is reading in her chair by the fire.

'Listen to this,' she says as I come in, her face all pink and red from the gas flames.

'*Beyond this place of wrath and tears*
Looms but the Horror of the shade,
And yet the menace of the years
Finds and shall find me unafraid.

It matters not how strait the gate,
How charged with punishments the scroll,
I am the master of my fate:
I am the captain of my soul.'

As Mum is reading I watch her face, half in shadow, half in light, and I think about how much I love her. She isn't mad and extravagant like my dad, or clever like Ms Hathaway, or giggly and silly like Leah. But before Dad died there was this horrible year when every time I turned the key in the door I wondered what I was going to find on the other side. And Mum felt like that too, and it was probably the hardest thing we've ever had to do, living like that. And Mum . . . she's a rock, like St Peter in the Bible. No matter how bad things get, she's not going anywhere.

'That's lovely,' I say, when she's finished, but I mean more than the poem.

Mum smiles. She looks down again, her thoughts already drifting back to her book. I say quickly, 'Mum?'

'Hmm?'

'Do you think Dad knew what he was doing? Or do you think he just did it because he was ill? Do you think he had a choice?'

Mum shuts the book. She takes off her reading glasses and folds them in her lap.

'Your father wasn't well,' she says at last. 'You know that. He wasn't thinking straight – and when you're unhappy, or angry, or frightened, sometimes you find yourself turning into someone you don't recognise any more – you know that as well as I do.'

I do.

'But, yes, I think he had a choice,' says Mum. 'Of course he did. We always do. No matter how hard things get, you always have a choice, Lizzie. And I'll never forgive him for making the choice he did.'

*

Do I forgive my dad? I don't know. I still love him. I want him back. But I'm angry with him too, so angry that I seem to spend half my life having arguments with him in my head, arguments where I tell him that he's selfish and cowardly and manipulative, and that Mum would never kill herself, no matter how crappy everything got, because she'd never leave me. And if Mum could do it, so could he. And that choice – what the church calls free will – is probably the coolest gift we've ever been given, ever, and that means that no matter how much fog there was, he didn't have to give in to it. He could have chosen to stay. If he'd loved us enough. And I know that's a melodramatic and self-centred way of thinking about it, and I'm not sure I really believe it anyway, because probably when things get that bad you *don't* know what you're doing any more, but I can't help it. It's what I think.

So, no, I haven't forgiven him. But I do understand how sometimes when you're unhappy all the colour sort of drains out of the world, and all the things you used to think were important get further away and out of focus. And I think maybe in that last year Mum and I got so out of focus for Dad that in the end he couldn't see how much we really mattered any more.

I don't forgive him for that, and one day I'm going to have to, I know. But I think I am starting to understand him, a little bit.

*

Saturday morning, Leah and I go ice-skating with a whole bunch of people – some guys from youth club, and the girls who sit with us in science, and a boy called Marky Phillips who Leah has fancied for ages and yesterday just got fed up of waiting around for and asked along. Leah and I are walking down our road to the bus stop, arm in arm, arguing as usual.

'Look,' I say. 'Say you get to purgatory—'

'Say I don't go straight to hell?'

'Yeah. Say God's having a good day and lets you off. Say you actually met Jesus – or God – or St Peter – and say they told you that you could get into heaven if you accepted Jesus as your saviour. You'd say yes, wouldn't you?'

'Can't I accept Mohammed as my saviour instead?' says Leah. 'Then I won't have to put up with my grandmother in the afterlife.'

'Leah!'

'Sorry! Sorry.' Leah scuffs her shoes through the fiery leaves all spread across the pavement. Winter's coming. Then she says, 'I think it would feel a bit weird, you know, having the glamorous and exotic life I'm planning on having – sleeping with all those film stars and being fabulously rich—'

'And then waking up and discovering you work in Tesco's?'

'Whatever, nun-girl. But wouldn't it be cheating? Not to care when you're alive and then give in after you're dead just to get into heaven?'

'You'll still pay for it in purgatory,' I tell her. 'Millions of years for film stars, probably.' I can't believe she's still arguing. No, actually, I can. Leah once came to school in sandals for an entire winter because her mother said it was either that or wear horrible hand-me-down shoes from her cousin. She's very stubborn. 'Please, Leah,' I say. 'Maybe I'm wrong and you don't go anywhere. If I'm wrong, who cares? But if I'm right, you'd be insane to say no. Wouldn't you?'

'*If* you're right,' says Leah. She sees my face and sighs. 'All right,' she says. '*If* I get to purgatory and *if* I see Jesus and *if* He manages to convince me I'm not having some weird hallucination, then fine. I'll do whatever He wants. Will that do?'

I suppose it'll have to.

Tonight, when I'm saying my prayers, I open my mind and hold it there in silence, listening for God. I sit on the edge of my bed, and as I sit, words come tumbling out of my head like sobs. *I'm sorry, I'm sorry, I'm sorry. I'm sorry,* I pray. *I'm sorry.*

I'm not sure who I'm apologising to. To God, for being so angry with Him? To Dad, for seeing only two ways of painting him – as a madman or a failure? Ms Hathaway says anyone can get to heaven if they accept Jesus as their saviour and if they're willing to put in their time in purgatory. Dad liked Jesus. He used to call him the Old Man. 'Why are you doing this to me, Old Man?' he used to say. And he'd cock his head sideways as though he was listening for an answer. 'He says: *Mind your own business, Joe, and get on with it.*'

I'm not worried about my dad and Jesus, but I am worried that God offered Dad the chance to go to purgatory, and Dad said no. Because those last months before he died . . . it was like he hated himself.

'I don't deserve you, or your mum,' he said to me.

I'm worried that he felt so guilty or unhappy that he really believed he deserved to be in hell. I've got another picture in my head – Dad, with his chin all stubbly because he hasn't shaven, leaning his head against the doorframe saying, 'I don't deserve to exist.' What if God offered him the way out and Dad was too lost to take it?

I'm sitting there with my palms together and the tips of my fingers pressed into my forehead and my breath warming the cold space between them, when I feel, well, I'm not sure exactly what I feel. It's like this sudden *jolt* of Dad-ness. All the things that made him him – his mad giggle, his bald patch, his anger, his music – all there, just for a moment, and then gone.

I jerk my head up and look around. There's nothing there. Of *course* there's nothing there. What am I expecting? Dad hovering over the bed in a halo and a bathrobe? But *something* happened. Unless I'm going mad. I think I have been going a little bit mad, this last year.

I try and think about it, but it doesn't make sense. If Dad was trying to send me a message, it was a pretty obscure one. Was he trying to tweak my nose? Make sense of that, Lizzie. Or just letting me know he was OK? Or what?

It's only later, as I'm trying to sleep, that I think about everything there was in that flash and I realise how much I'd forgotten about him. I'd remembered odd things about him; the way he cocked his head, his fingers all stained with tobacco from his horrible roll-your-owns, his head nodding in time to the music on the radio as he made me my sandwiches for school. And I'd remembered the bad things, the frightening things – the time he said we'd all be better off without him, or the time he stopped answering the phone because he thought the work should go to people who deserved it. But I'd forgotten the joy in him too. His face turned up to the sky, 'Look at those clouds, Lizzie! Look at that!' The way he tried to fix everything, even fiddly, complicated things he knew nothing about. The way he'd get interested in something – some new song, or bit of broken machinery. I'd be bouncing up and down, saying, '*Dad*, we're late. I was supposed to be there already. *Dad!*' And he wouldn't even hear me.

And I realise, of course he didn't go to hell. What was I thinking? You don't take illnesses to the afterlife, any more than you take dodgy legs or stupid hairdos. Dad hated himself because he was ill, and you can be lots of things in purgatory – angry, and proud, and frustrated, and stubborn – but if you don't have a brain, then how can your brain be sick? And I think of that spirit-flash I had, that clear, bright spark of intellect, and I imagine it up there in purgatory, poking the clouds to see how they stay afloat and wandering up to the angels, saying, 'Is that a flaming sword there? Really? How does that work?'

Glad we've got that sorted then, I think. And I pull the duvet tight around me, roll over and go to sleep.

CAN'T YOU SLEEP?

Frank Cottrell Boyce

CAN'T YOU SLEEP?

Miranda Okyere is: waiting for her test results. Fingers crossed!

Relationship Status: Married

Religion: Yeah, why not? Is this the moment to dismiss potential supernatural assistance? I think not.

Studied at: School – back in the day and far away.

Miranda likes these groups:

Looking at your status message from this time last year and realising you had no idea what was coming.

The awkward moment when: you hear someone put a cup of tea down next to your bed and you pretend to be asleep in a flirty way then realise you're not at home, you're in hospital, and the person you've been silently inviting into your bed is not your husband but the pierced and tattooed orderly.

Miranda has updated her profile.

Miranda is: in a good place right now.

Miranda likes:

Swimming costumes, swimming, jumping into a pool, climbing out of a pool.

Films: *The Swimmer, Doctor No, 10, Local Hero, From Here to Eternity, Dangerous When Wet.*

Books: *The Swimmer, The Beach, The Sea, Written After Swimming from Sestos to Abydos* (it's by Byron, baby).

Music: *Night Swimming* (REM), *Pure Shores* (All Saints), *You Better Swim* (Motorhead), *This Summer I Went Swimming* (Kate and Anne McGarrigle), *Sink or Swim – How You Gonna Know if You Don't Get In?* (The Waifs), *Wade in the Water.*

Billy Okyere commented on Miranda's music: What is happening here? I've checked this page every day since December 3rd 2011. Who updated Miranda's status? Whoever it is, you are sick. Plus you don't know anything about Miranda who had probably never even heard of any of those songs. FYI she loved Althea and Donna – Uptown Top Ranking. FYI do not update Miranda's Facebook. It's all I have.

Miranda commented:

I updated this myself. I love all these songs. Who is this? And who are Althea and Donna?

Billy Okyere posted a video.

Madeleine and Victoria singing Uptown Top Ranking on a rope swing. Victoria falls off in second chorus with hilarious outcomes.

Miranda and 22 others liked this video.

Miranda commented:

LOL. Great video. Thanks. Althea and Donna are younger than I expected.

Billy commented:

They are not Althea and Donna. They are our children. Miranda's children and mine. Miranda shot this clip. It was my birthday. Who is this?

Miranda was tagged in 658 photographs in the album 'Our Children' by Billy Okyere.

No comments

Miranda joined the group: The awkward moment when: you forgot about the existence of your own kids for like one nanosecond.

Billy poked Miranda.

Miranda posted a comment on her own wall:

OK. I remember them, ow. Sorry. Miss Forgetful! <— Blushing.

Billy commented:

I check this page every hour of every day. I've always

been dreaming that it would update. Now you – whoever you are – are updating it. How are you doing this? Why are you doing this? Who are you?

Miranda commented:

It is me. Miranda. I remember everything. Birthdays. Christmasses. First days at school. Everything. 658 different things.

Billy commented:

How can you be Miranda?

Miranda commented:

Same way you can be Billy. It's who I am.

Billy commented:

OK then. If you really are Miranda, tell me where you are?

Miranda commented:

Miranda is online.

Billy commented:

Online where?

Miranda commented:

In a good place. In a very good place. Like it says on my status update.

Billy commented:

You have to be sitting in front of a monitor to be online. What room is that monitor in? What can you see? Where are you, Miranda? I really want to know.

Miranda commented:

Friends. Photos. Tunes. Bits of film. Lists of stuff.

Billy commented:

Which friends?

Miranda commented:

Toby Floriston, Lola Alleyne and Angie Rowan.

Billy commented:

I've known Miranda since she was seventeen. I never heard her mention those songs, those books or those people. They are not her favourites or her friends. When you say LOL – are you really laughing out loud? Can you hear it? You must be sitting somewhere opening your mouth and letting a laugh out. Where is that?

Miranda commented:

No way do I understand one word of where this is going.

Billy commented:

If you're Miranda, when did you last see Billy? What was the last thing you said to me?

No Comments.

Billy poked Miranda

Billy commented:

Don't block me. Don't unfriend me. I need to talk to you. Whoever you are. I want to talk to you. The truth is I want to believe that you *are* Miranda.

Miranda commented:

I am Miranda. What are you talking about? What are you saying?

Billy commented:

Miranda is dead. 7.47 a.m. December 3rd 2011.

Twenty-five years ago. I've checked her Facebook every day since. Why would someone start to mess with it now?

No comments.

Billy poked Miranda.

No comments.

Billy re-poked Miranda.

Billy posted this video on Miranda's page:

Madeleine singing at her mother's funeral: a clip of Madeleine singing at Miranda's funeral – singing a lullaby which Miranda taught her, which Miranda had learned from her grandma in Ghana.

Billy commented:

I know you're not Miranda. I don't know who you are. But please don't stop updating / commenting / liking things now. It was good to see your updates. Even if they're not really you. When you first died, I rang your phone to hear your greeting. It was just the standard Orange one – not your voice – but it made me think of you. I checked your emails. It comforted me that spammers didn't know you were dead. You had stuff about mortgages and cheap flights and stuff from Lush. A few weeks ago your profile picture changed. I didn't comment. It was like . . . some sort of message or signal. I was holding my breath for more. I thought if I commented it might stop. Then you changed your likes and favourites. You deleted songs and books and things we shared. So I commented. And you stopped.

No further comments.

This comment could not be posted.

You are no longer Facebook friends with Miranda.

Miranda Okyere is: Dead

Miranda Okyere joined the group: Dead

Lola commented:

Hey. Welcome to Dead.

Angie commented:

We aren't actually dead. Something has happened to us but we are after all still commenting and posting and liking and so on. So we can't be dead.

Lola commented: We're not dead. We're immortal. Toby fixed it. Tell them, Toby.

Toby posted the following commerical video:

Is there life after death? Is there life after life? What comes next?

Insurance, a good diet, education, love – we work so hard to make this life better.

But we leave the next life to take care of itself.

Why?

On this Earth we live for our allotted span.

The next life could be a heck of a lot longer.

It could last forever.

Why leave it to chance.

Sheol Communications helps you to take charge.

Let Sheol be your shield.

Lola commented:

Toby made this place so me and him could be together. And he made other places so other people could be together. He spent his life making and selling after-lives. He made a fortune. And he made a heaven. Just for me. And him, obviously. And now you're here. You're our guests.

Lola is: loving Toby.

Toby is: loving Lola.

Angie commented:

Who is Toby?

Toby commented:

I'm Toby. I'm the one who saved your lives forever:

You spent half your life putting the other half of your life online – Facebook, Twitter, shopping accounts, emails. That stuff is indelible. Immortal. It stays in cyberspace after your body is gone. I came up with some software that keeps them active. Keeps them interacting. Growing. I made you your own personal heaven. Eternal Dream Homes.

Lola commented:

Thank you, Toby.

Angie commented:

Yes. Thank you, Toby. Very nice.

Miranda:

So we're dead, but we're still on Facebook.

Toby commented:

Why bring death into it. You've been upgraded to a more

durable version of yourself.

Miranda commented:

But didn't there used to be more to me? All I seem to think about is swimming and swimsuits. And not even swimming, just diving in and climbing out. I'm sure there was more. When I look around I can see comments and videos that have been removed. I was tagged in 658 photographs but they've all been deleted. All I can think of is getting in and out of a swimming pool. And there's a tune that goes round in my head...and a man who spoke to me...in here...about before. Billy. His name was Billy.

Toby commented:

Those things were upsetting you. So I removed them. I want us to be happy.

Miranda commented:

But you've removed bits of me.

Angie commented:

I must admit that grateful as I am to be resurrected from extinction, I too feel incomplete.

Toby commented:

Yes. That's because you've got no bodies. But I'm about to fix that...

Toby posted this free upgrade:

You can download 'Bodies' **here** (free).

Lola commented:

Look! Look! Look at me! I had so much trouble with my weight on the flesh side. Now look. Here I'm size six at most. Size six with boobs. I am literally in heaven. Miranda, you look terrible.

Miranda commented:

I was sick. I remember now. I was sick. That's why I'm wearing this headscarf. My hair fell out.

Lola commented:

It really doesn't work with that swimsuit.

Toby commented:

Your current bodies can be customised. Miranda, we can fill you out a bit . . .

Miranda commented:

Thanks. Wow! Boobs! They tickle!

Toby commented:

And let's give you back your hair. What would you like? You can have a 'fro if you like.

Lola commented:

And I feel a bit floaty and blurry and pixellated . . .

Toby commented:

You loved Audrey Hepburn when you were flesh-side, didn't you? And you only ever knew her as a bunch of pixels.

Lola commented:

Plus I'm thinner than her now. So this is clearly heaven.

Miranda is: crying

Angie commented:

Are you crying?

Miranda commented:

Sorry, sorry. It's just my hair. I really missed my hair.

I remember missing it. Thank you for my hair. I remember someone stroking it. I remember a tune that someone sang. Like a lullaby... Why did I lose my hair? Why did I miss my hair? What was going on?

Lola commented:

OMG, Angie, you're so old.

Angie commented:

I think that's because I lived a long time. That's why it's odd that I remember so little. Mostly just cutting out coloured paper, gluing things and a little bit about singing.

Toby commented:

Can everyone please refer to Angie as 'Miss Rowan' from now on?

Lola commented:

You were Toby's teacher. In primary school. He had a massive crush on you. That's why he wanted you here. But I don't think he wanted you old. I think he wanted you young.

~~Angie~~: Miss Rowan commented:

Yes, yes. Oh this is so very enjoyable. I'm eight years old. My knees should be a bit more scared and... that's it. I'm getting the hang of this now.

Toby commented:

If it's all right, Miss Rowan, I'd rather you were a bit older. I think you were about thirty...

~~Angie~~: Miss Rowan commented:

But I was so unhappy when I was thirty. I'd just discovered I couldn't have children...

Toby commented:

Actually it's creeping me out quite badly seeing you age eight. Can you age up now please?

Miranda commented:

Children. That's it. I had children. Children were in those photos. Maybe children made those comments. Children with names. Althea and Donna.

Toby commented:

This is all getting a bit gnarly. Remember, this isn't heaven heaven. This is *my* heaven. Let's drop the bad thoughts, shall we, and have a treat?

Download 'Panoramic' **here** (free).

Panoramic allows you to visualise your immediate online environment as an immersive but interactive landscape.

~~Angie~~: Miss Rowan commented:

Oh my goodness. Where are we?

Toby commented:

Welcome to Hyperborea – City of Frozen Spires. I imagineered it myself. The frozen waterfall over there is in fact a palace. Hundreds of rooms. Carpets of snow. Lifts powered by melt water. No need to worry about the cold anymore because you don't feel it...

~~Angie~~: Miss Rowan commented:

It's beautiful.

Toby commented:

Whenever I create something like this, I begin by

imagining myself back in Miss Rowan's class, staring out of the window, trying to think of something that would please you . . . that's what drives me on.

~~Angie~~: Miss Rowan commented:

In that case, I'm proud to be called Miss Rowan.

Toby commented:

Take a reindeer-skin coat – don't worry no reindeer were hurt in the making of this reindeer-skin coat. And Miranda, look what I have for you . . . down there, through the mist . . .

Miranda commented:

It all looks like some big arcade game. I hate arcade games.

Toby commented:

But look down there . . .

Miranda commented:

A swimming pool! I feel an overwhelming desire to dive into that pool, even though it's freezing.

Toby commented:

Ice that floats but doesn't feel cold . . .

The news from Hyperborea by Toby:

Lola is happy literally swanning around Hyperborea on a cute little ice floe pulled by swans. I'm hypnotised by the sight of Miranda – who was my swimming teacher and first crush when I was about eight – climbing out of the pool in a range of swimming suits. I used to sit on the side waiting for her to come out of the changing room and jump in, then spend the whole lesson waiting to watch her pull herself up onto the side. I would stand back and watch her in the showers. Now I have these pleasures more or less on a loop. I've managed to give her online self an incomprehensible pleasure in jumping in, climbing out and showering.

Miss Rowan even helped me make a mosaic portrait of her using bits of gummed coloured paper, which was heaven. We did this for maybe a year or so. Everyone was happy. Everyone got on. Lola did not feel threatened by these other women because they came from my remote past and were just childish crushes. She wouldn't let me have anyone I'd actually snogged, but she was happy to have all these crushes around. They are company for her in a way that the various dragons, unicorns and elves I've also got here are not.

But there is a reason that men fantasise about women. It's because real women are too complicated. No matter how you engineer them, they find a way of asserting themselves. Miss Rowan, for instance, has become agitated and returned to her theme of 'there was more to me than glue and coloured paper'. In fact, all of them – even Lola who owes me big time because in the end I did all this for her – complains from time to time about their 'incompleteness'. Miranda sometimes becomes quiet and sits on the edge of the pool, trying to recover a forgotten melody – which I'm worried may be in some way significant. Miss Rowan tried to cheer her up by sitting with Miranda's head on her knee, stroking her hair and singing her a medley of the songs she taught us in Reception. I like it, but I could see they were both experiencing vague, undefined feelings of dissatisfaction. I decided to address this issue by creating new experiences that we could all share here. New memories to distract from the old.

We built a new city together – a kind of El Dorado-themed jungle hideaway with talking jaguars and juggling monkeys. Miss Rowan made a model of it first with straws and balsa wood. It was fun.

We all learned to surf together, using telepathic dolphins as our tutors.

I realised that all of these were things that grew from my own interests and obsessions. So in learning to surf or forming a stadium band that played to 80 000 people from a stage positioned on a cumulo nimbus cloud I was letting them into my heart. Which I came to realise presented a security risk. The better they knew me, the more easily they might access my passwords.

It was time to look outwards. We all uploaded *War and Peace* together...

For *War and Peace* click **here**

Chandelier linen candelight samovar window laughter girl downy lip girl different card game money horse wolf horse wolf samovar loud male laughter bullets smoke clouds sky clouds sky sun moon sky Napoleon map Moscow boots cold walking Pierre snow snow snow

Miranda Okyere joined the group: I just read *War and Peace* and it rocked my socks.

Lola, Toby and Miss Rowan joined the group: I just read *War and Peace* and it rocked my socks.

For Anna Karenina click **here**

dressesuniformstrainslettersstationtraintraintraintrain!

Miranda Okyere joined the group: I can't believe that Anna Karenina died. Why did she do that?

News from Toby:

We are growing, liking new things, joining new groups. Our heaven is expanding and living. I think it's good.

News from Miranda:

By the time I post this I will not be any more. The lists, the likes, the pixels, they'll be deleted forever.

I'll miss the reading. I love the way you just 'click' and then a book bursts in – the colours and sounds, the way they fall like rain in your brain before they settle into patterns and shapes. And they stay there like memories of your own. It was a special feeling that those same shapes and memories were in Toby's brain and Lola's and Angie's. I felt closer to them.

But it made me wonder about something. A tune – there's always a tune on the edge of my mind, like a lullaby. That must be a memory. And it made me wonder – who else has that memory? Who do I share that with? I tried to chat about this in a one to one with Angie after she sang me those songs about the *Big Ship on the Alley Alley O* and the one about *Soldier Soldier, Won't You Marry Me?*. Music, she said, doesn't die. It just gets further away. I like to think of it moving out along all the nodes and wires and connections and hyperlinks, just tintinabulating through the synapses of the whole . . . then we got stuck. Our brains seemed to run up against a wall sometimes, like when you're surfing and you come to the bit where the sea and sky meet and you have to go back to the beginning.

Also about reading, and being closer and so on, it seemed to open doors for me. Not metaphorical doors, such as in Kafka, but real doors in the ice palace, which never seemed to open before. I realise what that is now. Toby shared all these fantastic experiences with us. Telepathic dolphins and so on. Because they were his inmost dreams and fantasies they were all, everyone of them, clues to him. He tried to keep his secrets but the more we did together, the more we became like him. Until one day I came to a locked door and I knew the password. Just knew it. As if it meant something to me. Juggling monkey, I said, and next thing I was through the door and in a gallery. Inside were some pictures as expected – pictures of me in swimming costumes for instance. But also spaces where pictures had once been and were now deleted. These were not just empty spaces on a wall. They were spaces. As if you had come to the place where the sky and the water meet but found a hole that you could climb through to the next level, or something.

I put the tip of my finger into one of the holes and instantly my finger was sucked out into a long long string – and the string was pulling at me from somewhere far away – like a wire or a current running into the furthest away place. I yanked it back just in time.

Exhausted I stood by the hole for a long time, thinking and listening.

Chatting one to one with Toby that night I told him a thought I'd had. It was just maths really. If he had had a crush on me when he was eight but then he had grown up, had a career, made a fortune and died, then that crush was a long time ago.

'Yes,' he said. 'Very long ago, but now it's back as fresh as paint.'

'I died before you did, Toby,' I said.

'Yes. And then I archived all that I could find about you. And when I died it came online and was active again.'

'How long is it since I died, then?'

'Maybe twenty-five years?'

This is when I realised that the people I'd known flesh-side were all grown up now and possibly dead themselves. 'But if they were dead,' I said, 'why aren't they in heaven here with me?' I "liked" them, after all. My grandmother, for instance, who taught me the tune which I have forgotten.'

'Because when all is said and done,' said Toby, 'this is my heaven. My heaven is real. The heaven your grandmother went to and your kids and Billy will go – those heavens might be all talk. It is the unknown. This is the known. It is possibly extinction whereas this is . . .'

He was going to say tinction. But he said, 'Forever. This is immortality and infinity.'

But all I could think was . . . Billy? What's Billy? The name sounded like the tinkle of a bell travelling towards me from far, far away. And a thought landed in my brain, sudden as cold – the thing that sound was travelling through – that was infinity. Not just more of the same. But something new and vast and impossible to imagine . . .

I spent a long time then, sitting by the holes, plucking up the courage to stick my finger in one. Wondering what it would be like to be yanked like a fish into the unknown. But after my finger unravelled for miles and miles, it stopped pulling at me. It connected with something and straight away the tune came flowing down my finger into my brain like light down a wire and into a bulb. And when, by that light, I could see names and faces all around me – Grandmother, Billy, Madeleine, Victoria – they flowed into me like the notes of a tune and they were all singing with me.

The tune was posted in group called *'Can't You Sleep?'* a sharing lullabies site. I 'liked' it. A woman had written *My dad used to sing it to me,* and I commented, *My grandmother sang it to me and I sang it to my daughter.* The woman commented, *My mother sang it to me, I think, but she died.* The woman's name was GoodasGold, but that's not her real name. She has a thumbnail by her name – she has a big 'fro, big smile. I could see all this through my extended finger.

I'm sitting here now, my finger stretched out and touching her thumbnail. I can sit here forever, commenting on her 'likes', liking her comments, watching her clips and listening to her playlists. Maybe she will add me and then she'll see my face and show it to her sister and they'll cry and shout, 'Mother we found you!' And I could watch over them.

But that is not how I will be with them.

Any second now I will put my whole hand into the frame that used to be a picture of what? The girls? Me? Billy? Playing, laughing. I'll be sucked out of here and all my lists will fly from me like birds frightened from the long grass and then the bright pixels of me will blow far and wide like from a dandelion, and the tiny bytes of me will settle into emails and comments and streaming, and when all those bytes and pixels have all fallen away, then I will tintinabulate forever like a tune. And Miranda will have left the room.

Can't You Sleep? – 1

BURYING BARKER

Keith Gray

BURYING BARKER

1

There's a spare seat on the bus on the way to school. There are fewer jokes about the teachers we like, fewer complaints about the ones we don't. There's a gap in the conversation while we huddle behind the main hall waiting for the first bell. There are more cigarettes to go round. There's one less name on the register as Mr Sanders calls for attendance. The chair in the back row by the window is empty. Because Marcus is dead.

Most mornings the form room's all bickering and noise. Chucked bags, rushed homework, borrowed lippy, teasing, flirting, reckoning. No one's particularly keen to settle in for the school day. But these past couple of days it was like a huge and heavy palm was pressing us down.

It might have surprised the new kid that we were all so quiet. He hesitated at the door; gripping his bag, not quite willing to take the plunge into a room full of strangers. He'd probably been hoping he could sneak in. But we all watched him. He glanced over his shoulder, back into the corridor, and I wondered whether he'd decided to chicken out and run for it, or if he was looking for Mr Sanders – a teacher to shield him.

This was going to be our first impression of him, he knew that. This was going to be a memory that stuck, a reference point, a single second of everlasting judgement. He hoped we'd like him, he hoped he'd make friends, hoped Megan or Sarah or any of us girls might even fancy him. He was worried he might make a dick of himself.

He was spic-and-span; combed, ironed, polished. His bag looked new. I imagined his mum had said to him, 'You need to make a good impression on your first day.' But she'd have been worrying about the teachers. He had dark hair cut short to hide the way it curled. I thought his forehead was too big. I thought his ears stuck out too much. He didn't look like my type. Simple instant impressions. He didn't look like a rocket scientist. Or a serial killer. And most of us in the class were probably thinking the same thing: he'd never fill that Marcus-shaped hole.

We stared at him. God, he looked uncomfortable. But he slung his bag over his shoulder and fixed a self-conscious glaze of *Whatever* on his face as he strode into the room. We watched him walk between the desks, heading for the only available seat – at the back, by the window.

'You can't sit there!' It was Jordy. He shouted across the room. 'That's Marcus's desk. You can't sit there.'

The new kid flinched. He glanced from Jordy to the empty chair and back again. Jordy met his look. But didn't get up. Yet.

I saw the thoughts scroll across the new kid's face. It was the only available seat. He wanted to sit down. He was desperate to sit down. All the attention burned. But what would the big lad with the elaborately flicked hair do if he sat in that chair? He looked over his shoulder towards the door. Again probably hoping Mr Sanders would appear.

'I'm telling you not to sit there.' *Now* Jordy was on his feet.

And maybe sat down with his teased and trendy hair you could be forgiven for not recognising the warning signs in Jordy Greene. But seeing him stand, seeing how he definitely didn't look like a rocket scientist, seeing how he certainly might be mistaken for a serial killer. Now was the time the new kid should have realised this was no game, or test, or taunt.

When he flicked his eyes around the room, searching everybody else's face for some thin rope of help, surely he should have understood that nobody wanted him sitting in that empty chair. He looked right at me, but I ignored him. For me, for *us*, that chair wasn't even cold yet. Maybe this afternoon, maybe after the funeral.

And then maybe never.

But the new kid made his choice.

'Marcus?' he called, thinking he was being funny, acting confident. Trying to be cool, but missing by a thousand miles. He made a show of looking around and under the desk. 'Marcus? He's not here, is he? I'll move if he asks me to.' He dropped his bag onto the desktop and slouched back in the chair.

Jordy shoved classmates aside to get across the room and at him in a single lunge. 'Get out of that chair. Move!'

Only with Jordy's shadow blocking his light did the new kid realise his mistake. But still he didn't get out of the chair. He was thinking he couldn't get up now. How bad would that look? Wouldn't it be even worse if he got up now?

No. It wouldn't.

'I said . . .' Jordy said again. But he'd never had much time for patience. He swung his closed brick of a fist into the new kid's face. It sounded like cannon-ball against glass.

I went looking for the new kid at lunch. He'd kept his head down all morning, and most people had ignored him right back. But he'd also kept his mouth shut when Mr Sanders had found him sprawled, bleeding, on the classroom floor. I thought he deserved an explanation.

I said to Jordy, 'He could have easily grassed you up. Maybe even got you kicked out.'

Jordy said, 'I'll email you when I give a shit.'

So I went looking alone. And caught up to him by the lockers on the second floor.

'Hey.' He didn't realise I was talking to him at first. 'Hey!'

When he recognised my face he tried to hurry away, taking his brand-new bag with him. It now had scuff marks and a Jordy-Greene-sized boot print from where it had been kicked across the room. I ran to catch him as he headed down the stairs. 'Wait. Listen. Don't you want to know why Jordy tried to break your nose?'

'Is it because he's an arsehole?'

'That has something to do with it,' I admitted.

I followed him outside into what the head likes to call 'the garden', even though it's just a concrete square with one lonely flowerbed in the middle.

It was a bright day – felt too sunny for a funeral.

The new kid tutted when he saw I was still behind him. He went to walk to his left, then turned to the right. Trouble was, this being his first day, he didn't have a clue how to disappear. He sighed when he saw I wasn't going to let him get away.

'Look,' he said. 'I know about his mate dying and everything. And that it was his mate's desk or chair or whatever. I'm sorry, seriously. You wouldn't believe how shitty I feel about it.' He pointed at his nose. 'But I've learned my lesson, yeah?'

The bruising under his eyes was a heavy purple, his nose was a mashed pumpkin. He wasn't so spic-and-span any more.

'Jordy and Marcus were best friends,' I said. 'And what with the funeral being this afternoon, everybody's a bit, you know...' I didn't like the bubble of emotion rising in my chest – I thought I'd done every last little bit of crying I could. I squinted up at the sun, deciding how I was going to say what I was going to say. 'Marcus was just always there, always right in the middle of whatever stuff was going on – good or bad. Do you know what I mean? He had lots of friends.'

The new kid shrugged.

I tried to hide the thick, wet click at the back of my throat. 'Everybody had a Marcus story.'

'Even me now,' he said. 'And I never even met him.'

I wasn't sure whether he meant it to be funny or not. But he said it with a lopsided smile, so I smiled too.

'Look, will you tell people that I didn't mean to be... That I feel stupid and, just, you know... Shitty.'

He was desperate for a second chance. 'I'll talk to Jordy,' I said.

'Tell him if I'd known, there's no way I'd have—'

'I'll talk to him. But I can't promise he's not going to want to hit you again.'

'Oh no, seriously, please. Tell him, not again. I mean, look at my nose after just one punch.' He jabbed a finger at it, rolling his wide eyes. 'See? My glasses don't even fit any more!'

And I laughed. It burst out of me, surprising me. It was such a Marcus-type thing to say. I supposed first impressions could be wrong.

He laughed with me, just a little bit. We stood awkwardly for a moment. 'I'm Dominic,' he said.

'Liv.'

He nodded. 'Have you got a Marcus story too?'

'Lots,' I said. 'I was his girlfriend.'

There are five wooden benches around the edge of 'the garden', all facing that lonely flowerbed in the middle. They have small silvery plaques fixed to the backrests, inscribed with old teachers' names (while students had etched their own names in the wood of the arms and slatted seat). Dominic and I sat on Mrs Kosca's bench.

Dominic was fidgety, self-conscious, sitting out in the open with me. Kids wandered by, some throwing evils, some just curious. He kept ducking his head or looking away from them. I guessed he was worried that by now everybody was going to know what had happened in registration. He was eager to go hide again. I wasn't going to let him. More and more I wanted him to understand why Jordy had hit him, why nobody wanted him sitting in Marcus's chair, why I kept needing to cry. And maybe it was for my sake more than his, but I wanted him to know something about Marcus too. I wanted to share a memory.

Marcus had a dog called Barker – had him since he was little. He was a massive, lolloping Yeti-monster of a thing. Marcus reckoned Barker was what happened if a golden retriever and Bigfoot had an ugly baby. And if you didn't like dogs, or were allergic or prissy and wouldn't let Barker jump and slobber all over you, then you were pretty much a weirdo as far as Marcus was concerned. My mum always knew when I'd been round at Marcus's house because my clothes were covered in dog hair. I cried too when I found out Barker had died because he felt a bit like my dog. But also, mainly, because I knew how devastated Marcus would be feeling.

It was a Saturday morning, last February. Marcus phoned to tell me, sounding awful. He'd said it hadn't been anything dramatic. It had happened sometime in the night, and his dad had found Barker curled up like he was sleeping that morning – so it was the surprise as much as anything. I'd told Marcus I'd go round to see him, but he'd said no, said he'd phone me the next day. But by half-ten that Sunday night I hadn't heard from him, and I wasn't worried exactly, just hoping everything was OK.

I texted him first. And when he didn't reply I called.

He answered on the second ring. He was all, 'Sorry, Liv. Sorry. Didn't mean to ignore you. Got my phone on silent.' He was whispering and I thought he might be trying to hide that he was crying. Then I realised he was panting, like he'd been running a marathon.

'Are you OK?'

'Can't really talk, Liv,' he whisper-panted. 'Sorry. Honest. Sorry, yeah? I'll call you back and—'

Then I heard Jordy in the background. 'Shit, Marcus. How deep is this? Your dad use a JCB, or what?'

I sat on the edge of my bed with my mobile pressed hard against my ear. There were other noises in the background too, but I couldn't work out what. Like thin thuds and muffled stomping. I was confused, but more curious. I knew Marcus well enough to know him and Jordy had to be up to something.

'Marcus? What—?'

He might have been about to fob me off, end the call, but he seemed to change his mind. 'Liv, you've got a spade, right?'

'A spade?'

'Spade, shovel, yeah? You've got a garden, so your mum and dad must have a spade, right? Jordy's place hasn't got a garden and my dad's only got this rusty, crappy thing. Definitely easier if we had two.'

'We should have one in the garage, I suppose. But, what—?'

'Great, brilliant. Really need it. Can you get it, bring it round?'

'Now?'

'Yeah, yeah. It'd be such a massive help, Liv. Honest, yeah? Really would.'

I couldn't work out what on earth Marcus and Jordy wanted with spades. Like you do on the phone sometimes, I tried to imagine what was going on at the other end of the line.

'Are you burying Barker?' I asked.

'No, no. Got to dig him up.'

I couldn't say anything to that. I let him listen to my stunned silence while I listened to Jordy's strenuous grunts and the thin thud of a spade splitting earth.

'You're brilliant, Liv,' he said. 'Honest you are. Just don't wake my parents when you come round, yeah?'

'But—'

'And a saw,' he said. 'If you find a saw too. Reckon it's gonna take two of them as well.'

With that he ended the call.

There's a real pleasure to telling a story. It's all about the listener. I watched Dominic as I spoke. He was only pretending to be interested at first – maybe felt guilted into listening. So Marcus had a dog, big wow! But the strange noises on the other end of the phone itched his curiosity. Marcus wanting a spade intrigued him. And the fact that the two of them were digging up a dead dog had him hooked.

'Digging up his dog? You didn't go and help, did you? What did he want a saw for?'

He was leaning forward, eager to know more. But he jumped, startled, and was on his feet when Jordy's bulk loomed over him.

I realised Jordy wasn't actually any taller than Dominic, just acted it. 'What you talking to *him* for?' he asked me.

'I'm telling him about Marcus.'

He curled his lip, unimpressed.

'About you two and Barker.'

He almost smiled. His mouth twitched with

the memory but he caught himself and shrugged. 'I wouldn't tell him anything.'

'I guess you'd just rather punch me again,' Dominic said, trying to sound cool and funny, glancing at me to see if I was smiling.

Jordy met his eye. 'Yeah,' he said.

And Dominic took a step away, banging the back of his legs into the bench.

Jordy said to me, 'The bus is here.'

I was surprised at the effort it took me to stand. Climbing to my feet felt horribly like climbing a mountain. The bus to take us to Marcus's funeral was waiting at the school gates.

I was scared the funeral was going to be the end. I didn't want it to be the final part – like the last chapter of a book, or a door closing shut. And maybe the beginning of forgetting. After today, and the finality of the funeral, there would be no more Marcus. Everybody would move on and the world would turn away. I didn't want to go if that was how it would be.

Jordy was already walking off but he looked back over his shoulder at me, waited.

Dominic said, 'I hope it goes . . .' But what could he say? How should a funeral *go*.

I forced my feet to move.

Dominic asked, 'Maybe see you tomorrow?' He was hoping he'd at least made one friend on his first day. 'You'll tell me what happened next? With Marcus and Barker. Even Jordy if you really have to. I'll meet you here.' He pointed at the bench. 'Mrs Kosca. Don't forget.'

'I'll try not to,' I told him.

2

We left the party early – Ali, Dominic, Megan, Liv and I. We found the nearest pub and squeezed into a booth near the back. It was bright and trendy inside, and Liv reckoned it used to be a hairdresser's or salon, or something, but the rest of us couldn't remember.

'Flickerz,' she said, drawing out the 'z'. 'That's what it was called. Come on, Jordy. For someone who used to spend so long on his hair, I can't believe you didn't have a map on your bedroom wall of all the hairdressers in town. With marked-out routes of the fastest way to get to them.'

Everybody laughed. And it was half-embarrassing, half-wonderful to be remembered this way. Especially because now, at the almost impossible to accept age of twenty-eight, that once-pampered hair was already evaporating from my temples. I'd always hoped there'd be at least a couple of years' gap between the end of spots and the beginning of baldness, but it didn't seem like I was going to be that lucky.

Still, I didn't think I was doing all that bad. At the reunion tonight there'd been too many people who looked scarily like their parents. Adrianne Kovack looked forty. Danny Daniels looked easily fifty! Some thin kids had become fat adults, while some fat kids had become thin adults. Some of them had their own kids. And that felt like the most bizarre thing in the world, even though it's the most natural thing in the world. Last time I'd seen Greg Fisher he was a needy nerdy gobshite with too many *Discworld* novels. Now he's an arrogant prick accountant with a kid with *Discworld* pyjamas. The kid didn't stand a chance... But Liv, well, she was still everyone's dream girl. She'd been a magnet all night long. It was disappointing she was way out of my league even now, but weirdly reassuring too. Thinking of everyone there tonight I'd have been most upset if she'd changed. She was a link to Marcus.

'Follicle masturbation,' I said. 'That's what my old man always called it when he caught me in front of a mirror.' I was happy enough for people to remember me as the kid with stupid hair, the poser, rather than as the kid with quick fists, the bully.

I guess that was one of the reasons I'd come to the ten-year reunion tonight. Yes, I wanted to see a couple of them again, and I guess I was curious about how people had turned out. But I couldn't help feeling I was also doing a bit of damage control. I'd changed. Luckily. And wanted people to know it.

Thing was, looking round the table, the two other blokes here, Ali and Dominic, I knew I'd battered them both in the past. I very much doubted they'd forgotten it, either.

Dominic was the one who made me squirm the most. His first day at our school and I'd virtually broken his nose. Not a great first impression. And maybe it was just the light in this place, but his nose still looked kind of crooked to me even now, his glasses a bit wonky.

I jumped to my feet. 'Right. Next round's mine. What're you having, Dominic?'

The pub was quiet. We'd doubled the number of customers, who'd all given us curious looks when we'd first walked in. They were all younger than us, trendier than us. We pretended not to care. The reunion's dress code had been black tie and I felt stuffy, claustrophobic in my suit. I reckon I'm the only man in the world that suits don't suit. I always end up looking like a bouncer. I noticed both Ali and Dominic had taken their ties off so gratefully took mine off too, rolled it up and shoved it into my pocket.

Megan said we should put some music on the juke box from 'back-in-the-day.' Even though Ali booed and Liv asked her not to, she still chose something she claimed used to be her favourite 'getting-ready-for-a-Friday-night-out song'. Whatever, I didn't recognise it. I guessed Megan was one of those people who wished she was still *back-in-the-day*. She was trying to squeeze her twenty-something self back into those teenage years, a bit like she was trying to squeeze her boobs and backside into that dress.

I changed the subject, asked her what she did now. She admitted she hated every minute of her IT call-centre job. 'Hate it hate it *hate* it.'

Ali told us about the restaurant he'd bought with his older brother and promised next time we had a reunion he'd make sure he provided better food than 'that nasty crap' we'd suffered at the school tonight.

'I thought you were going to be a film star?' I asked.

'Loads of time yet, eh?' he said, grinning.

Dominic was still aspiring to be a writer. He only shrugged when I asked him about it. But Liv said, 'It's good stuff. You should get him to let you read something.' I was surprised that she'd read something, surprised they were still in touch.

'What about you?' Dominic asked, changing the subject. 'What are you up to these days, Jordy?'

'I work with tough kids.' They looked intrigued. 'I'm a teacher, in a school for "bad lads".' I waggled my eyebrows to emphasise the quotation marks.

'Been teaching a few Jordy Greenes?' Ali asked. And got a few laughs.

'You're kidding,' I said. 'I maybe *thought* I was tough but I had nothing on some of these kids, believe me.'

'Bet you manage to slap them into line, though,

eh?' He karate chopped the air between us. '*Kapow!* The old Jordy Greene style.'

'I'm the new Jordy Greene these days,' I answered, maybe a bit too quickly.

'You're the *married* Jordy Greene,' Liv said. 'One day you'll have to introduce us to the woman who dared.'

Megan, who'd seemed a little tipsy only a minute before, had begun to take on the glazed look of the staggeringly drunk. She spilled her wine, swore, apologised. Swore again. Dominic went to the bar to get her a fresh glass.

'It's been so good to see everyone, hasn't it?' she slurred. 'Really, I mean. Properly, you know?' She was making a mess of mopping up the Cabernet with wet-wipes from her bag so gave up and just used a beer mat to scrape the puddle off the table's edge. 'We should all make a vow to keep in touch, shouldn't we?'

Liv laughed. 'A vow?'

'Oh yes, absolutely!' Megan looked like she'd forgotten it was her suggestion. 'Brilliant idea. Vow it, swear it. In blood. And if you break the vow you have to shag an ex-teacher as punishment.' She thought she was hilarious. She cackled like an orgasmic witch. Then threw her hand up. 'Bagsy Mr Sanders. He's still *gorgeous*.' With every sip of her wine Megan seemed to lose a year or three, until she was once again the loud teenager I remembered a little too well.

Dominic came back with drinks for everyone. We all pretended to say, *No*. We made a show of saying, *We shouldn't*. But we did anyway and knocked back the previous round in our haste to get on with the next.

I noticed Dominic switch seats as he sat down. He'd started the night next to Ali but had manoeuvred himself to get elbow to elbow with Liv. I had nothing against Dominic, not now, but reckoned he'd have to be King Super Lucky of Fortune Island to have any hope of getting anywhere with Liv.

But what the hell? Good luck to him.

'So which teacher would you choose, Dominic?' Megan asked. 'Who was your favourite?'

He took a sip of his beer while he thought about it. 'Mr Mohan,' he said. 'Remember him?'

We all burst out laughing. He hadn't heard Megan's run-up to this particular conversation and looked kind of non-plussed by our reaction. Mr Mohan had been a fusty old duffer even back then.

'He's the only reason I passed English,' Dominic said, pushing his glasses up his nose. 'I thought he was all right. As long as he kept his shoes on.'

Megan gave such a sudden loud snort I thought twin jets of wine were going to shoot from her nose. 'Cheesy Mo! That's what we called him. I had him for English in Year Nine and he'd stink the whole class out. He always did it, didn't he? He'd take his shoes off and sit there with his feet up on his desk, flexing his toes in these bright green or orange socks. It was *rank*. And can you remember one day somebody took in a gasmask or something, didn't they?'

Ali nodded. 'Last day of term. Cheesy Mo went apeshit, eh? Didn't just hit the roof, went through it.' Ali made the noise of our old teacher rocketing through the classroom ceiling loud enough to draw stares from the younger, trendier clientele in the pub. We ignored them.

'Jesus, I wonder what happened to Cheesy Mo,' Megan said. 'He wasn't there tonight, was he?'

'He's got a bench in the garden,' Liv said.

That shut us up. We sipped our drinks guiltily.

But not for too long. 'Hope the smelly bastard keeps his shoes on in heaven,' Ali said. Which kind of set us off again.

'...I'm definitely choosing hell if he's up there...'

'...stinking out all the poor angels...'

Now that we were on the subject of death it was only a matter of time before someone mentioned Marcus. I made sure it was me.

'And you know who it was had the gasmask, don't you? Marcus. This old World War Two thing he'd got from God-knows where.'

'Had to be Marcus,' Ali said. 'You were really tight with him, right? Best mates, eh?'

I nodded.

'I could never work him out,' Ali said. 'Was he trying to get into trouble on purpose, or did he just not get that not everyone thought he was funny? He never seemed to "switch off", you know what I mean?'

'He was sweet when you got him alone,' Liv said. 'When he wasn't performing.'

And even now, twelve years since he'd died, all this time later, I still found myself wanting to defend him, my best friend.

'I always reckoned his head was too small for all of the stuff going on inside it,' I said. 'Some days I'd be with him and it was like he was going to burst or explode if he didn't squeeze out some of what he had crammed up in there.'

'I missed him,' Megan said. 'Well, obviously, still do. Obviously, right? He was my first kiss.'

That made us all laugh. Ali howled and drummed the table.

'In the nurse's room,' Megan said. 'When I broke my leg in Year Eight. I was crying, really *beeling*. It was *so* painful. He just walked in and said he'd been sent to kiss it better. But he kissed me on the lips.'

'He was your first as well, wasn't he, Liv?' Ali asked. 'Not just kiss though, eh?'

'Leave it,' Liv said in a way that made Ali howl again and the rest of us laugh harder.

'What about the dog story?' Dominic asked her. 'You promised me you'd tell me what happened, and you never did.'

Megan and Ali hadn't heard it, either. Liv looked at me, 'You tell it,' she said.

I wasn't able to tell it exactly the way I remembered it in my head. I did my best, but the real memory's better, sharper, truer.

It's this freezing cold Sunday night in February and we're at the bottom of Marcus's long back garden, underneath the apple trees or pear trees or whatever they were, digging up his dog, Barker. And the ground's rock hard. Marcus's dad had only buried Barker the day before, but it had rained and frozen and rained and frozen, and I just couldn't believe how hard that ground was.

I was sweating and swearing and Marcus was all, 'Shush. Quiet. Don't wake my mum and dad, yeah? They'll go mental.'

He kept kind of squatting to peer out from under the branches or darting in front of the greenhouse to look back at his parent's window. He reckoned his dad was paranoid and said he kept all these baseball bats hidden in different places around the house – under beds, in wardrobes, behind the sofa – in case of burglars. He was worried his old man was going to come charging down the garden, swinging a bat in each hand.

We only had this one spade between us and had to keep swapping over. But then Liv turned up with another one. I can't remember if he'd phoned her, or she'd called him.

She said: 'I've looked like a right weirdo walking the streets at night with a garden spade.'

'Maybe people thought you were carrying it for protection,' Marcus said. 'In case of rapists, yeah?'

'If you're really doing what you said you were doing on the phone, then I doubt I should have brought it at all.' She waited for us to answer. I just kept on digging. 'You're not really digging up poor Barker, are you?' Again she waited. Marcus made a kind of um *sound. And she turned on me, 'Oh, Jesus, Jordy. What the hell are you letting him do this time?'*

'Don't blame me.' I just kept digging. Why was I here? Why was I helping? Marcus was my best friend. What other reason was there?

Liv was disgusted, then curious. And then disgusted all over again. Marcus got her to hold the torch. I was sweating hard despite how cold it was. Poor Liv was shivering pretty bad. But it didn't take us too long after that to dig down far enough to find Barker.

He was wrapped in one of Marcus's mum's best bed sheets. Which had caused a row, he said. It had been white but was now caked in mud and dirt and crushed worms. And that dog weighed a ton. I'd thought the digging was the tough part, but Barker was massive and it took both me and Marcus together to drag him out of the ground.

Liv kept saying how stupid and mad and wrong this was, but she didn't try to stop us. I reckoned she was curious again. But I was beginning to wonder if I could do this, go through with it all. The sheet was stiff with the cold and the dirt and we had to kind of peel it off. It got stuck to the fur in places and we had to rip it away. The worst part was that Barker still looked like Barker, but really, obviously dead. We laid him down on the grass on his side. He didn't look like he was sleeping. He was too dead for that. His lips had drawn back from his teeth, as though he was snarling, and I could see the tip of his tongue, which was black and dry and weirdly scaly looking. His eye was half-open, but looked more like a marble, like it would make a tink-tink *noise if you tapped it.*

Liv said, 'This is horrible, Marcus.'

'It's what he would have wanted.'

'You know that, do you?' Liv asked. 'He told you, did he?'

'He was my dog, yeah? So I know, yeah?' He crouched down beside Barker and tickled his ear. He tried to close that half-staring eye but the lid was stuck. 'Can I have the saw?' he asked.

'I didn't bring it,' Liv said.

Marcus sighed. 'Come on, Liv. Look, honest. This is exactly what he would have wanted. It's what I'd want, yeah? Definitely.'

Liv folded her arms.

'Liv, please. My dad's is broken. We need yours.'

'I'm cold,' I said. I wasn't joking. It felt like my sweat was starting to freeze to me. 'And I'm in for a massive bollocking if my dad sees I've snuck out again. If we're doing it, then let's just do it quickly.'

Liv was far from happy. She pulled the saw out of the plastic bag she'd dropped beside one of the apple trees. 'I don't want it back. Not after this.' It was a backsaw with a bright-blue handle, looked new. 'This is the grossest, most disgusting…'

Marcus darted a look at his house. 'Shush! Come on, Liv. Quiet, yeah?'

'Are you going to do it here?' she asked.

'Don't know where else to take him. What d'you reckon, Jordy?'

'It might be kind of loud,' I said. 'Drag him as far back as possible. Behind the greenhouse maybe.'

So Marcus took Barker's front legs while I grabbed hold of the back ones. Without the sheet wrapped around him I was surprised his fur still felt soft. I could smell him now too. It wasn't a strong smell, but kind of spicy, and you couldn't help catching a small whiff as we struggled with him. He smelled like bad pepperoni.

We left a trail in the frosty grass as we dragged him but couldn't be seen from his parents' window once we got behind the greenhouse.

'OK,' Marcus said. 'We should be OK here, yeah? Put him down gently.'

And that almost made me laugh. Gently. Like forgetting totally what we were going to do next.

'He needs to be in five bits,' Marcus said as he crouched beside the dog with Liv's hacksaw in his hand. But then swore and pulled a face. 'Yeah. Sorry. Not really thought the next bit through properly.'

We stared down at the dog in the moon-shadowed grass.

'Saw's not big enough, is it?' It'll never get through him.' He measured the saw against Barker's torso. Then his neck. 'Could get his head off though, yeah?'

Liv turned away. 'Jesus.'

'Five parts, right?' I said. 'Why not just do his legs and leave the rest of him here? Be the easiest.' I really didn't like the idea of holding Barker's head while Marcus sawed away at the neck.

Luckily Marcus nodded. 'Yeah. Yeah, OK. That'll work. Do his back ones first, OK?'

I took a breath, tried not to think too much about what we were doing. Failed. So just held my breath as I grabbed one of Barker's back legs.

'You don't have to watch,' Marcus told Liv.

'Too fucking right I don't,' she said with her back to us. But I noticed her shoulders flinch, hunch at the sound the saw made.

The leg juddered, vibrated in my hands. Marcus cut with hurried rasps which sent small but sickening pins and needles through me. I wanted to forget I was holding Barker's leg but I could feel his fur. I was happy there wasn't much blood – it glooped, didn't spurt, then trickled and soon stopped altogether.

Liv still had her back to us. 'How can you not even begin to think this is the most utterly vile and repulsive . . .?'

'It was what he would've wanted,' Marcus said again. He was panting slightly with the effort.

'He was a dog! He wanted to eat sausages, shag your granny's poodles, chase ducks.'

'Exactly,' Marcus said. 'That's exactly it, yeah?'

'He didn't want sawing into little bits by a demented fifteen-year-old. Tell him, Jordy.'

I stayed quiet. I was concentrating on keeping my Sunday dinner down.

'You say that, yeah?' Marcus said. 'You say that, but how do you really know?'

The leg came away suddenly. I'd been holding it so tightly I staggered backwards, almost falling over on my arse when Marcus at last cut all the way through. I back-peddled to stay upright. Then realised I was waving the severed leg around as I tried to stay balanced. So I dropped it. And then fell over.

'One down,' Marcus said. 'Three to go. D'you want to do some sawing?' he asked me.

'Reckon it's best if you do it,' I told him.

He nodded. Bent over the other back leg. 'Tougher than it looks, yeah?' He wiped the sweat out of his eyes.

Megan puked. I wasn't sure if it was my story's fault or the drink. She kind of coughed it up in a sloppy sputter. She tried to catch most of it in her wine glass.

Liv, Dominic, Ali and me leaped to our feet to avoid it. The barman scowled at us. The younger drinkers laughed at us.

'Maybe we should get going,' Liv said.

'I still haven't heard the end yet,' Dominic said. 'Come on, please? What happened?'

'I went home at that point,' Liv said. 'I'd about reached my level of repulsiveness for one night.'

Megan groaned. She was seriously green. She shuddered, heaved, but this time nothing came up.

'She's a ticking barf-bomb,' Ali said. 'We should get her home, eh?'

'Somebody's got to tell me what happened!' Dominic wailed.

Liv helped Megan to stand. 'Next time,' she told him. 'Promise. We'll get together again soon.'

He seemed happy with that. Happy that there was a chance of seeing Liv again, anyway.

Liv and I managed to manhandle Megan out onto the street. It was a warm night but spitting with rain. Hit by the fresh air Megan heaved into the gutter, her hands on her knees. Liv held her hair out of her face for her. Us three blokes stood with our hands in our pockets, feeling awkward.

Megan wiped her mouth with a tissue. 'Have I made a real fool of myself?' she whispered to Liv. But she was so drunk it was kind of a loud whisper and we all heard it despite the traffic.

'Don't worry about it,' Liv told her. 'Let's get you a taxi.'

'But I have, haven't I? I've not seen any of you for years and now this is all you're going to remember about me.' Megan followed the old drunk's cliché. From sick to self-pity.

I flagged down the next taxi I saw. We all said it had been good to see each other. Hugged. Said we'd definitely keep in touch this time. I hoped we all meant it, I really did. Liv helped Megan into the cab.

Dominic said, 'I'm on the way. Is it OK if I share?'

Ali and I raised our eyebrows at him, and he was decent enough to blush, but chose to ignore us. The three of them drove away.

Ali turned up the collar of his jacket against the drizzle. 'Well, memorable, eh? And good to know after ten years some things don't change. Dominic's still chasing Liv. Megan's still eighteen.'

'Reckon so,' I agreed.

'You've changed, though, eh? Not so *mean-Jordy-Greene* any more. Helping tough kids? You've changed, man. Big time.'

'I'll take that as a compliment,' I said.

The rain was getting heavier.

'I left nearly a full pint in there,' Ali said, hooking a thumb at the bar behind us.

I grinned. 'Me too. Let's go finish them properly. And I'll bore you with stories all about the new caring-sharing Jordy Greene.'

'Sounds good to me.'

And with that we hustled back inside.

3

I'd thought I was going to die. Twice. Once, when I went over my bike's handlebars and saw the ground rushing towards me. And twice, when I hit it.

I think I got the life-flashing-in-front-of-my-eyes thing in the split second between the two. But I'm only eleven, so there wasn't that much life to see.

Anyway, I landed on my face. Ripped open my cheek in a burning, grazing blaze of bloody mess. Burst my bottom lip like a hot grape. Tore off half an eyebrow and lost it in among the streaky red and fleshy skid-mark I left on the road.

Now I'm stitched and gauzed and bandaged. I look like a mutant.

And I'm in two minds. Maybe I'm glad I didn't die, because now I can get more of a life, more memories and stuff, so that when the real flashing-in-front-of-my-eyes thing happens I might actually get to see something interesting. Or maybe I wish I was dead because tomorrow's my first day at Stonner Secondary School and, by the way, *I look like a mutant!*

It's not going to be a great first impression.

Dad was doing his best to be *Dadly*.

'When I was your age—'

I turned back to my computer. I hated it when

he said that. Things had changed. Amoebas had evolved. I wanted to scowl but it hurt my face too much.

Luckily Dad could guess the face I'd be pulling without me actually having to do it. He sighed, sat down on the edge of my bed and had to talk to the back of my head.

'Mum says you've decided not to go to school tomorrow.'

'I can't.'

'I don't think—'

I spun in my chair so he could see. I gave him the full one hundred per cent horror of it.

'I look like a mutant!'

Unbelievably, Dad laughed.

I wanted to glare at him, but glaring hurt even worse than scowling.

'See! If even my own dad laughs . . .'

He held up his hands, trying to say sorry, and wrestled his smile into a twisted grimace.

'I'm sorry, Callum. Just . . . Look, mutant's pushing it a little, don't you think? The doctor said you'll be fine in a couple of weeks. And if you are left with a tiny scar, that'll seem cool, right? Every scar tells a story.'

'You want me to be scarred for life? Great. You'll be happy if everyone tomorrow thinks I'm a freak.'

'You're not a "freak", either.'

'First day,' I said. 'My very first day at secondary school and I've got to go looking like this!'

I turned back to my computer. I had the camera set up so I could see my mutant face full-screen.

'No way. I'm not going. I can't!'

He just didn't *want* to get it, purposely didn't understand. Secondary school was the place I'd be a teenager. I was scared I'd not meet the right people or make the right friends. I had to be in with the right crowd so I didn't get bullied or ignored or laughed at. I needed to meet people who liked the same things I liked. Or find out what the right things to like were and make sure I got to like them too. I'd hopefully get my first girlfriend, and then have my first kiss and stuff. It was all one hundred per cent too important to mess up on the first day. And my face was going to spoil everything.

'Mum'll make you go,' Dad said.

'No she won't. She can't.'

'She's scarier than me.'

I nearly scowled again, but caught myself just in time.

Dad stood up. Hanging on my wardrobe door was my brand-new, spic-and-span, never-worn-before Stonner Secondary School uniform. He brushed pretend fluff off the blazer's shoulders.

'It's just my school *costume*,' I told him.

He nodded. I was glad he understood that much at

least. When he went to work he wore what he called his 'office costume', even though Mum said it was an expensive suit. But dad didn't enjoy his work much and he said his suit made people think he was something he wasn't. Deep down he wanted to be a writer. He'd invented a detective character called Max Krakow, but Mum said I was too young to read any of the books yet. And I was starting to think that if they ever got published I'd probably be too old.

'Is being worried about how you look the only reason you don't want to go tomorrow?' Dad asked. Slyly, I thought.

'It's enough, isn't it?'

He shrugged. My dad was a great shrugger. Inuits may have one hundred words for snow, but my dad could make a single shrug mean a million things. You needed an app to translate them all.

'See my nose?' he asked. He took his glasses off and pointed at it. 'The kink? I got that my first day at a new school. I met this boy called Jordy Greene who gave it to me.'

I knew my dad had a kink in his nose, and had known even when I was a little kid that not everybody's dad did. But I realised I'd never wondered how come. I suppose I'd never thought there might be a *reason* for it. It had just always been part of him. Forever.

'You got beaten up?'

'In a manner of speaking.'

I was shocked. Then embarrassed. Why was my dad such a wimp?

Like father like son, I guessed. I decided to blame his genes. The wimpy ones he'd passed on to me.

'So you got beaten up on your first day at a new school? And that's meant to make me feel better about tomorrow? Thanks, Dad. Brilliant.'

I saw him begin to laugh again. But this time I scowled no matter how much it hurt my stitches.

'OK, sorry,' he said. 'Maybe I'm telling the story wrong.'

'First impressions aren't all they're cracked up to be,' Dad said.

He was sitting on the edge of my bed again, talking to the back of my head again.

'I changed school when your granddad got a new job and we moved. It was rough, kind of nerve-wracking. I had to start in the middle of term, I didn't know anyone, and was so, *so* desperate to make a good first impression, I ended up making a complete idiot of myself.'

'One hundred per cent still not helping,' I told him.

He sighed. 'I sat in a dead boy's seat. Marcus. He'd died a couple of days before and everybody thought of me as a bit of poor substitute, I guess.'

I had no idea where this was meant to be going.

'Is this real? Or is it *Max Krakow*?' I asked over my shoulder.

He smiled. 'It's definitely real. Fortunately.'

I was completely lost. What did a dead kid from back in the Stone Age have to do with me?

'Did Marcus have a face like this?' I spun round so I could give him the full horror again.

He didn't even blink. 'Don't know. Never met him.'

'So why—?'

'Even though I never got to meet Marcus, I often think I'd like to be a little bit more like he was.' He did one of his famous shrugs. 'People still remember him, still talk about him. There's this one story about when he chopped his dog up into different bits.'

I really, absolutely, one hundred per cent didn't know what to say to that. And I think it showed on my face.

On the first day of primary school Marcus made two best friends: Jordy and Barker. Jordy was the boy who sat next to him in class and Barker was a dog.

Marcus's mum hit Barker with her car on the way to that first day at school. It wasn't her fault, the dog ran out into the road in front of her. Marcus said she was crying and shocked and shaking. Between them they managed to pick Barker up (he was big even as a puppy) and put him on the back seat. They drove him straight to the vet's.

Of course, back then, Jordy didn't know any of this. He admits himself he was a chubby, anxious five-year-old sitting in his brand-new school uniform wondering how come everybody else had somebody to sit next to in the class except him. And then, after an hour or so, he thought: how come the boy at the desk next to him was late, had tears in his eyes and blood on his white school top? The teacher wasn't even mad at him for being late, but she did make him stand in front of the class and tell everybody what had happened.

Marcus, apparently, told the story brilliantly. He made it exciting, edge-of-the-seat stuff: the dog bleeding, whining, and the way his mum had sped to the vet's, even shooting through two red lights. And a cheer went up from the class when he said that, despite a broken leg, the dog had survived. Then Jordy was happy that Marcus was sitting next to him. He was the most famous person in class.

The teacher told them to tell as many people as possible what had happened, and to ask around, so they could find the dog's real owners. Jordy helped with the search – sort of. He and Marcus didn't try as hard as they could have because Marcus had already persuaded his parents to allow him to keep the dog if nobody showed up to claim him. And that's how Jordy and Marcus became best friends. Jordy kept Marcus's secret of the half-hearted search.

They were still best friends ten years later when the dog, Barker, unfortunately died.

Marcus's dad did a good job of burying Barker in their back garden, and the whole family had a solemn doggy funeral, but it wasn't enough for Marcus. He felt Barker deserved something more, something special. And Marcus, being Marcus, knew exactly what that special thing should be.

He persuaded both Jordy (who, in all honesty, wouldn't have needed all that much persuading) and his girlfriend to help him out. In the middle of the night they dug Barker up and cut him into five separate pieces – cut off his legs, but left the rest of him intact. They reburied his body underneath some trees in Marcus's back garden, stamping down the mud, hiding that they'd ever dug him up in the first place. Marcus had a plan for each leg.

The first leg was the easiest. Next-door but one was where Mr Bell lived. He was an old man well into his seventies but he'd always had a soft spot for Barker. There were days when Barker wandered off of his own accord and nine times out of ten he'd be found along the street at Mr Bell's, and Mr Bell bought extra sausages for those occasions.

Marcus's parents were quite strict about what Barker could eat, only buying 'proper' dog food and vet-recommended treats (which Marcus always suspected tasted like a dog version of Ryvita, or other cardboardy health-stuff). And Barker was fine eating that kind of stuff when he had to. But he knew he'd get the butcher's best if he made his way to Mr Bell's. If he was lucky, and nobody realised he was missing quick enough, Mr Bell would even cook the sausages for him.

So Mr Bell's was the first place Marcus and Jordy went on that cold February night. They hopped over the fences in between and silently dug a hole under a rose bush at the very bottom of the old man's garden. That's where they buried Barker's left front leg.

Marcus didn't think it was good enough that Barker only got to be buried in one place. He said Barker had different places he loved when he was alive and should get to be buried in all of them, so he was in his favourite places when he was dead too. It made a strange but perfect sense to Marcus.

So the second place the two friends sneaked to was the park behind the school. Marcus said Barker was never happier than when he was pissing off the ducks; running at them, barking as they flapped, chasing them into their pond. But never quite catching them.

Climbing the gates into the park was dangerous. They had to be careful not to clang their spades against the metal railings. If they got spotted by a passing car...

'What the hell do we tell someone who asks us what we've got in the bag?' Jordy wanted to know.

'Don't tell them anything,' Marcus replied. 'Just run, yeah?'

They'd never been in the park after the gates were locked, after dark. It was pitch-black. They crept through the trees, almost having to feel their way. They could hear the ducks chuntering and grumbling close by, but couldn't actually see them. They only knew they were at the pond's edge when Jordy put his foot into it with a loud splash. He swore as his trainer filled with freezing water.

'We should bury the leg as close to the pond as we can,' Marcus said. 'It'll be like Barker's forever keeping a watch on the ducks. Forever keeping them on their toes, yeah?'

'Ducks don't have toes,' Jordy told him. But Marcus didn't care.

Two legs left, and the next one was going to Marcus's grandma's house. It was after three in the morning by the time they got there and Jordy's wet foot was cold enough to make penguins shiver. The plan had been to sneak alongside the house and round to his grandma's back garden, but her gravel drive was as loud as any alarm. Marcus dived behind a hedge as the security light flared, Jordy scrambled beneath the old lady's car. And only a second later Bella and Romy were barking fit to burst.

They were his grandma's pampered poodles, who

Barker had lusted after and slobbered over. Marcus believed part of him would want to be buried with his 'girlfriends'.

Jordy stayed close to the ground as he peered out from under the Fiat Panda. He couldn't see Marcus anywhere. Bella and Romy's barking sounded so loud; high-pitched yaps stabbing at the silent night. He knew Marcus's grandma was deaf, but her neighbours probably weren't. If they didn't do something quick they'd be caught for sure. He slowly dragged himself across the gravel to crane his neck as far out from under the car as he dared.

Marcus was at the garden gate, urging him to follow as he ran off along the street.

When Jordy caught him up Marcus said over his shoulder, 'I buried it under the front hedge. It's good enough. He's still close to them, yeah?'

'As long as you did it deep enough,' Jordy said. 'You don't want the poodles digging him up.'

Then maybe he wished he hadn't said anything because Marcus went back and risked everything all over again to dig a hole twice as deep.

At last they took the remaining leg (the back left) to Barker's final resting place. And this was perhaps the riskiest of all because it wasn't behind a hedge or in the middle of a pitch-black park but right out in the open. Marcus said the leg should be buried at the place he first met Barker, which was the corner of the road where his mum had hit the dog with her car all those years before.

Two, three cars passed them as they dug. They worked quickly. Who knew what the drivers thought these two kids were doing digging up the grass verge at four in the morning. Jordy and Marcus kept their backs turned and their heads down.

'You gonna say anything?' Jordy asked him as Marcus solemnly placed Barker's last leg into the hasty, rough-edged hole. 'It's a funeral, sort of, right?'

But Marcus shook his head. 'I said it all to him when he was alive. That's the important thing.'

A fourth car passed as they were filling in the hole again, flattening the ground down. Marcus swore, shouted that it looked like a cop car. It was coming back! But neither of them hung around long enough to see if it really was the police. They were too quick to disappear down the back streets with their spades clutched tight in their hands.

Of course, I didn't believe anybody would ever really do anything like that.

'Definitely all sounds a bit *Max Krakow* to me,' I told Dad.

He did one of his annoying shrugs. 'It's the truth,' he said. 'As it was told to me.'

'So you weren't even there?'

He shook his head.

'How do you even know it's true, then?' I couldn't help feeling smug when I said it. I'd backed him into a corner now.

So I was shocked when he said, 'Because your mum was there. She told me.'

And the shock showed on my face. Making it hurt.

He opened my bedroom door and called downstairs, 'Liv! Liv?'

But when Mum came up she wasn't happy Dad had told me the story. She sighed at him. 'Did you have to?' She busied herself picking up dropped socks and folding a crumpled jumper I'd left on the floor. 'I'm sure there are plenty of other stories you could have—'

'You cut up a dog?' I asked. 'That's gross, Mum. One hundred per cent disgusting.'

She sighed again, giving Dad a brilliant glare. 'I can assure you I didn't do any cutting. I had no idea what they were—'

'Look,' Dad said, holding his hands up for peace. 'The point is . . .'

And both Mum and I waited for the stunning shot of wisdom.

He shrugged. 'It's all about the stories you leave behind, isn't it? Who cares about what first impression you give at school tomorrow?'

'I don't care because I'm not going,' I said.

'Yes you are,' Mum told me.

'I made a right idiot of myself the first time I met your mum,' Dad said, pushing his glasses up his nose. 'But first impressions don't last. You're worried about tomorrow, but it's only one day. You've got quite a few years to leave a real, lasting impression.'

'But—'

Dad was back on the edge of my bed. 'But, it's the memories you make and the stories that get told. Nobody's going to tell stories about me in my "office costume" typing nonsense into a computer all day from nine to five. I mean, I really hope not. If you want to believe there's such a thing as an afterlife, then it's the stories you leave behind. That's what I believe immortality is. Marcus is immortal because someone, somewhere, will always be telling a story about him.'

I knew we never went to church, but: 'Don't you believe in heaven and hell?' I asked.

Mum said, 'Maybe hell is being forgotten.'

'You never met Marcus?' I asked Dad.

He shook his head. 'Doesn't matter. I'm still sitting here keeping him immortal.'

There was another question that was bugging me. 'Do you know if, when he died, his friend Jordy cut him up too? Like Barker, I mean? And buried bits of him in different places too?'

Leaving my parents speechless was always a novelty.

But it made one hundred per cent sense in my head.

'Well,' Dad said at last. 'I suppose he is, kind of. Maybe nobody cut off his arms and legs exactly, but the stories about him are buried in plenty of different people's heads. You could say I've just buried a piece of him in yours, couldn't you?'

'And if you tell someone else,' Mum said. 'And they tell someone else…'

I nodded. I liked this version of immortality. And maybe my face would heal…Eventually.

Mum and Dad seemed pleased too. Dad stood up and Mum slipped her arm round his back. They looked like they'd just won a merit badge in good parenting or something.

'Still doesn't mean I'm going to school tomorrow,' I told them.

Mum said, 'We'll see…'

But Dad just shrugged.

ABOUT THE AUTHORS

I have been a fan of **Julie Bertagna's** writing for many years, in fact ever since her first novel *The Spark Gap* way back in 1996. She has always written vivid and distinctive stories set in the here and now, such as the Scottish Arts Council Award-winning *Soundtrack* and Booktrust Teenage Prize shortlisted *The Opposite of Chocolate*. But it was setting her sights on all our futures with her Drowned World Trilogy that brought her the most attention. The opening book *Exodus* was described by *The Guardian* as 'a miracle of a novel' and went on to be shortlisted for the Whitbread Book Award. *Zenith* and *Aurora* completed the trilogy and all three have won Julie floods of fans from all around the globe.

One of the UK's most imaginative writers for young people right now is **Jonathon Stroud**. The Bartimaeus cycle of books (so far a trilogy plus a prequel) about an irascible, egomaniacal 5000-year-old djinni, have racked-up a Quill Award nomination for Best Children's Chapter Book, an ALA Notable Book Award, a Child Magazine Best Book of the Year recommendation, the Prix Millepages, and between them are a New York Times bestselling series. My personal favourite book of Jonathon's is *Heroes of the Valley*, a dark but witty and inventive spin on some old Norse myths, and reading it I knew that asking him to contribute a story for this collection he'd come up with something genuinely unique.

Philip Ardagh is funny. It's a fact. And he's a man whose beard travels First Class. He's the award-winning author of the Eddie Dickens adventures, which is currently available in over thirty languages, as well as the Unlikely Exploits and Grubtown Tales series. He also collaborated with Sir Paul McCartney on the ex-Beatle's first children's book. Philip's non-fiction titles include *WOW! Ideas that Changed the World*, *Why are Castles Castle-Shaped?* and *Philip Ardagh's Book of Absolutely Useless Lists for Absolutely Every Day of the Year*. I was lucky enough to meet the man himself in Dublin last year and he told me how much he enjoyed writing short stories. 'Oh really?' I said. 'It's funny you should say that...'

Books For Keeps has described **Gillian Philip** as 'an intelligent writer making intelligent demands of her reader, crossing genres with confidence.' Her stand-alone novels include *Bad Faith*, *Crossing the Line* and *The Opposite of Amber* – perhaps labelled as thrillers, but each praiseworthy for its distinctiveness and ambition. *Firebrand* was the first book in her Rebel Angels series and it swept up both fans and critics alike. It was nominated for the David Gemmel Legend Award while *The Times* called it 'The best children's fantasy of 2010 . . . fantastically violent, utterly thrilling'. *Bloodstone* is the equally impressive follow-up. Not content to rest on anyone's laurels, Gillian can sometimes be found moonlighting as Gabriella Poole, the author of the Darke Academy series.

Malorie Blackman is without doubt one of the best-loved and most successful writers for young people working in the UK today. *Noughts & Crosses* and its sequels are arguably Malorie's most successful books, but with *Hacker*, *The Stuff of Nightmares*, *A.N.T.I.D.O.T.E.*, *Cloud Busting*, *Boys Don't Cry*... the list of incredible titles goes on and on. Malorie's books have either won or been shortlisted for just about every award going, while the TV adaptation of *Pig-Heart Boy* won a BAFTA and a Royal Television Society Award for Best Children's Drama. In 2005 Malorie's outstanding and distinguished contribution to British children's literature was recognised with the Children's Book Circle Eleanor Farjeon Award and in 2008 she was honoured with an OBE.

Sally Nicholls published her stunning, moving debut about an eleven-year-old leukaemia sufferer, *Ways To Live Forever*, when she was only twenty five. The book was shortlisted for the Branford Boase Award, won the Waterstone's Children's Book Prize and touched thousands of young people, walking away with several regional awards as voted for by the readers themselves. In 2008 Sally was named the Glen Dimplex New Writer of the Year. The book's success continued when it was filmed, winning several awards for the director and screenwriter Gustav Ron. Sally's more recent novels are *Seasons of Secrets*, which has its roots in the folk tales of the pagan god of summer, and *All Fall Down* which whisks the reader back to 1349 and the Black Death.

I've often wondered if **Frank Cottrell Boyce** is the UK's hardest-working writer. Not only has he written episodes of the TV soaps *Brookside* and *Coronation Street*, as well as over a dozen movie screenplays (*24 Hour Party People* being a personal, nostalgic favourite of mine), he's also produced some of the finest books for children in recent years. His first novel for young readers, *Millions*, won the CILIP Carnegie Medal. His two subsequent novels, *Framed* and *Cosmic*, were both shortlisted for the prestigious medal as well, while more recently *The Unforgotten Coat* won the Costa Children's Book Award. He also wrote *Chitty Chitty Bang Bang Flies Again*, the official sequel to the much-loved Ian Flemming children's story. And luckily for us he somehow managed to find the time to contribute something rather special to this collection too.

My first anthology for Andersen Press was *Losing It* in 2010, which tackled the prickly subject of virginity, and what on earth to do with it. My novels for young people include *Creepers*, *Happy*, *The Runner*, *Warehouse*, *Malarkey*, *The Fearful* and *Ostrich Boys*.

Keith Gray

LOSING IT

edited by
Keith Gray

Will you, won't you? Should you, shouldn't you?

Have you . . .?

A gift? Or a burden?

MELVIN BURGESS, ANNE FINE, KEITH GRAY, MARY HOOPER, SOPHIE MCKENZIE, PATRICK NESS, BALI RAI AND JENNY VALENTINE.

Losing It is an original and thought-provoking collection of stories from some of today's leading writers for young people: some funny, some moving, some haunting but all revolving around the same subject – having sex for the first time.

Everything you ever wanted to know about virginity but your parents were too embarrassed to tell you.

9781849390996 £5.99

HAUNTED

A FANTASTIC COLLECTION OF GHOST STORIES FROM TODAY'S LEADING CHILDREN'S AUTHORS

'A chilling slice of horror. An excellent balance of traditional and modern and a perfect pocket-money purchase for winter evenings.' *Daily Mail*

Derek Landy, Philip Reeve, Joseph Delaney, Susan Cooper, Eleanor Updale, Jamila Gavin, Mal Peet, Matt Haig, Berlie Doherty, Robin Jarvis and Sam Llewellyn have come together to bring you eleven ghost stories: from a ghost walk around York; to a drowned boy, who's determined to find someone to play with; to a lost child trapped in a mirror, ready to pull you in; to devilish creatures, waiting with bated breath for their next young victim; to an ancient woodland reawakened. Some will make you scream, some will make you shiver, but all will haunt you gently long after you've put the book down.

9781849393218 £6.99

The Cry of the Wolf

MELVIN BURGESS

'A writer of the highest quality with exceptional powers of insight.'
Sunday Times

It was a mistake for Ben to tell the Hunter that there are still wolves in Surrey. For the Hunter is a fanatic, always on the lookout for unusual prey. Driven by an ambition to wipe out the last English wolves, the Hunter sets out on a savage quest. But what happens when the Hunter becomes the hunted?

'A disturbing book, but of real quality; you will applaud the end.'
Observer

'A Dickens of the future.'
Michael Rosen

Burning Issy

MELVIN BURGESS

'Are you frightened of dying, Issy?'

Issy doesn't know where she came from or who she is. Night after night, she has the same nightmare: she burns in a fire and at the heart of the flames is a face she dare not look at. Fear and superstition are everywhere. She must run - from the Witch-finder, from the evil hag who wants her, from those she loves and maybe even from her own true nature...

'Vivid and atmospheric ...
Unforgettable stuff'
Guardian

'Brutally honest ... this remarkable historical novel erupts into life from the very first page.'
Financial Times

9781849393973 £5.99